SIERRA MESA

To Art,
— who is a walking, talking, living, breathing history of the Middle Border and a man I've esteemed since I was knee high to a Hyde County grasshopper.

Best wishes,

[signature]

Nov. 1994

SIERRA MESA

JERRY TIPPENS

NPI

Northwest Publishing, Inc.
Salt Lake City, Utah

NPI

Sierra Mesa

All rights reserved.
Copyright © 1994 Northwest Publishing, Inc.

Reproduction in any manner, in whole or in part,
in English or in other languages, or otherwise
without written permission of the publisher is prohibited.

This is a work of fiction.
All characters and events portrayed in this book are fictional,
and any resemblance to real people or incidents is purely coincidental.
For information address: Northwest Publishing, Inc.
6906 South 300 West, Salt Lake City, Utah 84047

SCM 07 19 94

Edited by R. Larsen

PRINTING HISTORY
First Printing 1994

ISBN: 1-56901-256-3

NPI books are published by Northwest Publishing, Incorporated,
6906 South 300 West, Salt Lake City, Utah 84047.
The name "NPI" and the "NPI" logo are trademarks belonging to
Northwest Publishing, Incorporated.

PRINTED IN THE UNITED STATES OF AMERICA.
10 9 8 7 6 5 4 3 2 1

To Helen with love and admiration.

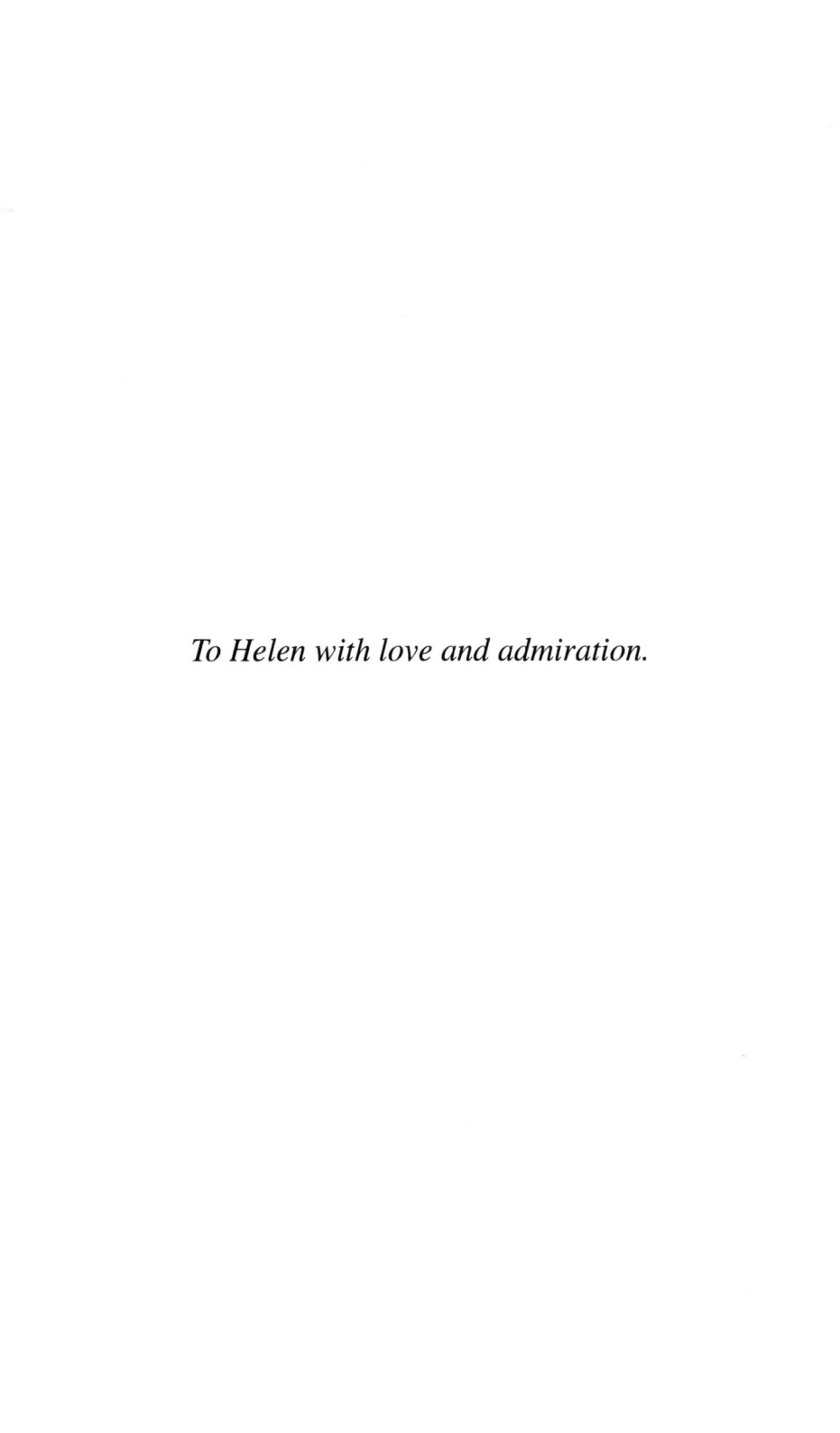

ONE

First came the homesteaders. Then came the railroad. Then came statehood.
You'll agree that was a lot of upheaval to cope with over the course of a few short years. Somehow, however, Sierra Mesa and the ranching community around it survived each calamity as it came.
But we almost didn't survive Emory G. Pastwell when he hit town.
They were definitely the best of times and the worst of times back there in the wackiest year I've ever known. But for sure this is not a tale of two cities. Sierra Mesa and Hampton City were only small towns and barely that.
I was just a strapping young lad at the time and had that English author, Charles Dickens, still fresh in my mind. The

school marm, Miss Bordelyk, had just assigned the seventh and eighth graders to read *The Tale of Two Cities* when the weird events began to unfold.

That's probably why I always think of the Dickens story when I look back on a scheme that nearly doomed Sierra Mesa and almost turned a barren piece of the high plains into a bustling city.

Hampton City would have achieved that lofty status only at the expense of Sierra Mesa, which would have been emptied of its businesses and its people and left for nothing but a ghost town. Of course, that was all right with some people. They were only too eager to trample on the grave of Sierra Mesa.

Up till that spring, things in these wide open spaces had pretty well settled down. It is true that before my time, my family and some of the other ranchers had had a bit of a dispute with the Indians over who got to use which land. But the issue eventually was resolved, fairly or not, and there were several years of tranquillity in a region that was getting to be mighty calm and peaceful to be called the Western Frontier.

The storekeeper, Henry Guzman, had come up from the southwest somewhere. He claimed he had learned enough Spanish to appreciate the beauty of the language and he would give his country store a pretty Spanish name. He called it the Sierra Mesa. The name stuck as Mr. Guzman's general store grew into a small town.

The folks around here became right proud to have a nice sounding Spanish name for their address. Nobody thought much about what Sierra Mesa meant, if anyone knew enough Spanish to realize that a sawthoothed tableland was in reality a contradiction of terms. They just enjoyed it.

They had a town with a musical ring to it, something different while everything else around them seemed to have plain old names, like Gortonville, the county seat of Jefferson County. The only exceptions were the few communities or geographical features that bore Indian identifications, like Minnehaha or Sacagawea or Cheyenne or Shoshoni or Missoula.

As Sierra Mesa took root and grew, eventually another

general store and a blacksmith shop joined Mr. Guzman's store. A barber came to town. We even got a law office of sorts. Then a rich-looking fellow from the East came in and opened a bank. A weekly newspaper soon followed. A few other little stores took hold, more or less specializing in things like clocks and jewelry, or furniture or saddlery. These were the things that were to some extent excess baggage in the general stores.

Pretty soon a new store concentrated on hardware and another on clothing. A doctor hung out his shingle. A drugstore followed hard on his heels.

The general stores weren't so general anymore. Gradually they focused mostly on groceries, although they kept an assortment of all the other items around just out of habit, I guess, or to be ready in case the new shops folded up and old times came back. The livery stable and blacksmith shop were located next to each other. As time went by both of them started selling equipment to farmers and ranchers and gradually each took to going by a fancy new monicker, farm implement dealer.

We had three churches and four saloons. It probably should have been the other way around. The churches tended to the spiritual needs on Sunday morning and the bars to the need for spirits on Saturday night.

It was those spirits on Saturday night that reduced the number of souls seeking the spiritual on Sunday morning, although what went on on Saturday night sometimes should have meant more people in search of redemption on Sunday morning.

Of course if all who should have would have attended, it would have meant sanctuaries crowded with sinners in all three churches, the Catholics, the Lutherans and the Methodists.

The Methodists were really not just Methodists but seemed to be a collection of all manner of Protestants who weren't Lutherans. Hard-shell Baptists went there, grumbling that it would have to do until they could have their own church. The family of Unitarians attended, with a suspicious eye on everyone around them. Episcopalians, Congregationalists and Presbyterians worshipped with the Methodists while dreaming of the more appropriate services of their own someday.

There was one Jewish family. We felt kind of sorry for them, for there wasn't a synagogue or a rabbi for hundreds of miles in any direction. Every once in a while they would show up at one of the Christian churches on the theory that God was God and they would worship as best they could. They would take from the service what they could get out of it and try to be tolerant of what came after the faiths parted company a couple of thousand years ago. Mostly, though, they tended to their own spiritual needs at home and I guess they got kind of accustomed to it.

That's about the way Sierra Mesa stood, taking good care of the provisions and services for a well-established ranching community for twenty to thirty miles around it. Our lives had become so stable and tranquil we may have been caught off guard when the whole community got tossed around by the triple turbulence of homesteaders, railroad and statehood that seemed to wallop us all at once.

With all of that happening all of a sudden, you have to admit that our community took it in stride about as well as people anywhere could.

The homesteaders changed the nature of the land, but after a while the ranchers got used to them and even decided that it wasn't such a bad idea to put up fences, too.

The railroad wouldn't have come if the homesteaders hadn't got here first and had to get crops to market. But the ranchers finally figured out it was nice to have a railhead right near home. It made it a lot easier to move the cattle to market than to make the long drives they used to make.

Statehood meant that it was even more dangerous to have the legislature in session than it was in territorial days.

True, the governor was elected now, but apparently he was still more obligated to the same old big shots than to the people who elected him. Nonetheless, we learned to live with legislators and the governor and the powerful people to whom they always seemed beholden.

All the hub-bub of course meant some strain on Sierra Mesa. More businessmen were looking for opportunities and more people were looking for a town to live in. But mostly they didn't think Sierra Mesa had the touches of respectability they preferred.

It wasn't laid out right, with straight streets marked off in regular blocks. Sierra Mesa had just kind of grown, hit and miss, with no particular design. New folks wanted to give streets names like Iowa or Indiana, making ties to where they had come from. But Sierra Mesa didn't have street names; nor did the original horse trails that came to serve as streets lend themselves to names.

Except for the disappointment of the new people to the town, though, things were going pretty well. Before it had grown too much, the people of Sierra Mesa did incorporate their town as a city under territorial law. They thought they would have a better chance of controlling its future that way. It seemed appropriate that Henry Guzman was elected the first mayor.

All in all folks in and around Sierra Mesa adjusted pretty well to a whole lot of change that hit them hard and fast.

But even after the homesteaders, the railroad, then statehood, we weren't prepared for Emory G. Pastwell.

TWO

Out in the country we heard about the strange event after it happened. Dad had to make a quick trip to town one day for something that couldn't wait until Saturday and he came back telling about the doggonedest dandy from the East you ever did see. As soon as the opportunity arose, which was, of course, Saturday, the whole family piled into the wagon and went to town so we all could see for ourselves.

Sierra Mesa had been visited by traveling men before. They came slicked down and wearing their Sunday-go-to-meeting clothes right in the middle of the week. They wore those heavy suit jackets even on hot summer days and always choked themselves on some kind of fabric tied around their neck, no matter how uncomfortable it must have felt.

Emory G. Pastwell operated on a higher plane. He was a

traveling man, all right, but he outdid every other traveling man Sierra Mesa had seen when he stepped off the Great Lakes Pacific train at the station on the edge of town where the new rail line was built.

A lot of town folks always went down to the station when a train was coming in so as not to miss the excitement. The moment he stepped off, they sensed there was an aura about him that designated him as something special, or at a minimum that he thought he was. At the least he was good for entertainment.

He wore a taller gray top hat than anyone in Sierra Mesa ever imagined. He had on a gray suit, but it wasn't like other traveling men's. The coat had long tails that reached down below the backs of his knees. He had on a vest under the coat and a big, bright gold watch chain across it.

Everybody wondered what such a man could want in Sierra Mesa. He had to be a peddler, but what was he peddling to dress like that in these parts? He carried no sample case or elixir bag. Mr. Pastwell didn't let on anything when he stepped off the train. He bowed and tipped his big hat to all the ladies, shook hands with all the men and offered them long, dark cigars and inquired about the finest hotel in the town.

It was easy to oblige him on that one. Sierra Mesa only had one hotel. Oh, one of the saloons used to rent rooms, which initially were intended for pleasures of the flesh. But the saloon keeper quit trying to rent his rooms when the hotel was built right after the railroad came in. So it was new and close by. Whether he liked it or not, Mr. Pastwell never indicated to the contrary.

He hung around town for a few days and never once mentioned what he was selling, which you'll have to concede is mighty unusual for a man in the business of selling. He just asked a lot of questions about the area.

Wherever he went he asked the same questions. He asked them in all four saloons. He strolled through the stores inquiring as he went. He would stop people on the street. He sought out the clergy for advice.

"How many people would you say now live in Sierra Mesa and the trading area around it?" he would inquire.

"Oh, maybe three, four thousand. Yeah. I'd say gettin' close to four thousand now. Must be close to a thousand right here in town. Eight, nine hundred anyway. Gettin' kinda crowded around here."

"About how much has the area grown since homesteading started?"

"Oh, counting the country folks, it's about triple in size."

"What would you guess it's going to grow from now on?"

"Well, that's kind of hard to say. But people still seem to be coming in."

"You happy with things the way they are or would you make changes if you could?"

That's where the answers varied.

One would say: "I'd touch a match to the blamed town and start all over from scratch."

Another would say: "Can't think of anything. I'm pretty satisfied with the town as it is."

Now, Sierra Mesa had heard questions like that before from businessmen considering locating their businesses there. So maybe the dude wasn't a peddler after all, but was interested in a business. In the past, however, the others made no bones about why they were interested. When the rich-looking fellow from the East intended to open a bank, he said so. If one was thinking of a livery stable he acknowledged as much.

But Emory G. Pastwell gave no indication at all what kind of business he had in mind. Every day, though, when he made his rounds of the town he was dressed in the same fancy way, so those of us who only heard about him on his arrival got to see him in full attire for ourselves when we got to town.

One Sunday afternoon on a gorgeous spring day, he rented a horse and buggy from the livery and headed west out of town. That's the direction we live. Fact is, I spotted him when I was out riding around, checking to see if Becky Fullmer was also free from chores and able to play for a while.

We were still of an age when boys weren't supposed to like

girls and girls weren't supposed to like boys, although we were only a couple of years from the time when boys suddenly really liked girls and girls really liked boys.

But Becky and I didn't have much choice. We were the only kids close enough to play with. We were next-door neighbors, living just three miles apart, and were the same age. We started as the only first graders together in the one-room school over yonder and now we were the only seventh graders. So circumstances made pals of us whether we were supposed to be or not.

Actually, we were more like a family than neighbors in many ways. We were the Baxters. My dad and Becky's dad had grown up on these same ranches their fathers had started. They were boyhood friends. Later they cowboyed together until a couple of young women, who were girlhood friends, decided it was time to settle down a pair of young buckaroos. So my folks, Ben and Nellie Baxter, and Becky's folks, Ted and Sally Fullmer, wound up taking over from their parents.

Our place was nine miles west of Sierra Mesa and a mile south. The Fullmers were eight miles west and a mile north. So, with just three miles separating our homes, we lived particularly close together.

A few homesteaders lived closer to one another, and the people in town were jammed together tighter than the house from the barn. We always felt sorry for the town kids having so little room to run around in. Becky and I couldn't understand how they stood it. Still, we were glad our houses weren't farther apart. They might have been, for it was rare for ranch homes to be located within three miles of each other.

Becky's and my favorite place was a spot near where our rangeland and their rangeland came together. The railroad was built dangerously close to it, but didn't spoil it for us. In fact, it gave us something else to watch from the sanctity of our hiding place.

There was a draw down low where a creek ran in the spring. Along a large swamp-like area by the creek, horseweeds grew in wild profusion every year.

Other places kids may have had forests to entertain them. As a matter-of-fact, some were not so terribly far away. We could see the mountains off in the distance. We knew they were covered with trees and were very green, but from here they looked a far-off blue-gray leaning toward black. The foothills probably started only about thirty miles away, but for all the good that did us they might as well have been a thousand.

On the prairie, there weren't too many trees. A few willows and cottonwoods by some of the creeks, maybe, but for us the horseweeds made our forest. They grew straight and tall twelve to fourteen feet every year, and they were just about as thick as the hair on the mane of the animal they were named after.

They were our target this day. Early each spring Becky and I would plan the trails and campsites we wanted among the horseweeds all summer long and on a nice day we'd go out and clear them out while they were little and easy to pick. By the time school was out the rest would have grown up while leaving our trails and campsites open for our special purposes.

An old corral from days forgotten was rotting away by the creek, all overgrown by horseweeds in the summertime. We liked to play around it and it gave us a handy place to tie up our horses. Up the hill a ways was a hole in the ground. There used to be a country store on the spot, but it burned down and left just the cellar.

That fire is what sparked folks several years ago to go looking for another storekeeper and that's what brought Mr. Gutzman up from the Southwest to open his store, which of course was the beginning of Sierra Mesa.

Becky and I would poke around the old cellar by the hour, marveling how that hole in the ground might have started a town if a fire hadn't started first.

It served us especially well the day when Mr. Pastwell drove out our way. I heard Becky's meadowlark signal about the time she heard my imitation of a coyote. She always impressed me with how she could sing the meadowlark's song better than the bird itself and I wished I could master the coyote's howl half as well. Regardless, the signals served us suitably as our special code.

We met at an easy lope at the old corral. We left our horses and sneaked up to the hole in the ground. We were going to map our strategy for our horseweed forest for that summer, but Mr. Pastwell distracted us. First we had to figure out what he was doing out there by himself.

It wasn't that we were doing anything to be ashamed of really, or that we suspected Mr. Pastwell was up to anything wrong or suspicious. We were just curious, but didn't want to butt in. Besides, it was sort of a game for us to have a view of the world from the sanctity of our hiding place. From the old cellar we could peek out and see that he pulled up at the fuel stop the railroad had installed on the range. It was the first railroad stop out of Sierra Mesa, maybe eleven miles from town and about a mile from our hole in the ground.

He looked around for a bit, and that was all. He didn't even get out of his buggy. For all our sneakiness, we didn't see him do a thing but look, which hardly satisfied our curiosity at all. But that was all we got for our trouble before he headed back to town and we turned our attention to the horseweeds at hand. The next day without letting on a thing to anyone he got on the east-bound train, taking his secret and our puzzlement with him.

But he wasn't gone too long and over time we eventually learned what it had all been about. In the turbulent months that were to follow, however, we were often in the dark about what this traveling man was peddling. When one thing became clear, there likely was something else that hadn't reached the surface yet.

It turns out that what he peddled best was a line a mile long to Miss Emily Hampton, which occurred only a few months before we saw him poking around the fuel drop.

Like so many of the young people who lived in Rensburgh, she thought of her life as pretty boring. Chicago may have been only about thirty miles away, but, like our mountains, it might as well have been a thousand. In other words, Rensburgh could just as well have been Sierra Mesa to the kids stuck there.

Even though the Great Lakes Pacific Railroad was headquartered in Rensburgh and gave them a direct tie to Chicago, the young people of Rensburgh never, or hardly ever, got to get aboard to take in the bright lights and the mysteries of the big city. Thirty miles or a thousand made no difference if you couldn't get across them.

So when the traveling man came to Rensburgh with his display cases of fine garments for the clothing stores, he found a ready and willing listener in a pretty, young woman working in one.

Emily Hampton, he sensed, was easy prey. She was already twenty-two, still unmarried and had no prospects in sight. Oh, there were many young men in Rensburgh who were willing prospects, but none that she could stand. The idea of spending a life with any of them, caring for his home, sharing his bed, raising his children, was repulsive to her. Moreover, here she was in a dead-end job in a dull town. There had to be something more to life.

The dark days of winter were the worst. The holidays provided some diversion from Rensburgh's mundane ways. But once they were over, the miserable days of January and February just underscored how Rensburgh squeezed all the pleasure out of life.

Emily may have thought of herself as far too sophisticated for the silly boys of Rensburgh, but she was out of her league with the smooth-talking salesman. He easily filled her head with wonders of the cities to which he routinely traveled. He spoke as though the adventures she could barely imagine were normal to his exotic lifestyle.

"Why, in Chicago," he told her, "the day is just beginning when the sun goes down. You don't go home from work and figure that's all there is to life until another day as dull as the last one starts the next morning."

Emily had always figured it was so. But what did they do when the day began at sundown, she wondered, and she caught herself blurting it out like a little child.

"What all do they do when the sun goes down?"

"You can go to the theater. They have theaters as big as the whole city of Rensburgh. Or to a night club. They have night clubs with singing and dancing and fine food and fancy drinks open all night long."

"I suppose you can just walk around and look at it all."

"'Course. Or you can stroll in the parks or by the lake. Or better, get a fancy cab with big horses all decked out in harness that looks like it came from a jewelry store and ride in high fashion through the city."

"Yes, yes." She was eager for more, her eyes shining as she fixed her vision on all the excitement just thirty miles away.

"Sometimes you can join a big crowd and hear a senator or a mayor give a speech. Or, you like pretty clothes. I can tell just by looking at you. You can go to the style shows in the big dress stores and check out fashions that come right from Paris."

She was enraptured. "What do you do when you're in Chicago?"

"Sometimes one. Sometimes the other. They're all there to do. It wouldn't work for you because you're a lady, but I often go to the prize fights or in the summer watch the Chicago team in the National Baseball League."

"Oh, I like games. I like to watch baseball. I really do."

"Why don't you go check Chicago out for yourself? It's right next door."

Radiance turned downcast. "Oh, I want to. I always wanted to. But my mother won't let me. Neither would my father when he was alive. My brother backs up Mother. He says Chicago is no place for a young lady to be."

"Nonsense. Chicago is exactly the place for a beautiful, sophisticated young lady like you. You come with me and I'll show you just how much fun Chicago can be." By afterthought he added, "For a young lady, that is."

The trap was set. The lure of Chicago would be too great for a girl from Rensburgh to resist.

"When you get off work, come by my hotel. I'll show you the maps and we'll check out the train schedule and we can make plans. We'll see just how well it would work for you to see Chicago."

Somewhere in her subconscience a conscience no doubt was speaking frantically to her. But she wasn't heeding the caution. Chicago was calling. And so was the chance to see it with a dashing, handsome man, far more thrilling than any of the juvenile boys around Rensburgh.

So she arrived at his hotel. Even in her frame of mind, she knew people wouldn't understand a lady meeting a gentleman in his hotel room. She glanced around furtively, but after all she wasn't doing anything wrong. Just learning about Chicago and how to travel there.

He was waiting. And he was ready. He ushered her into his room and removed the wrap she wore against the January cold. Then he took her firmly into his strong arms. Startled, she looked at him uncertain what to do. She started to resist when he kissed her hard on the lips.

She groped for the defenses she had been building since before puberty, but found her resistance quickly fading as she felt his probing, demanding tongue against her tongue and his hands caressing her body. She had no defenses left when he began to unbutton her blouse. Her nipples, already hard, tightened even more to his touch as his practiced hands bared her breasts. Her senses were aflame as he deftly unfastened her long skirt and removed it. Any sense of propriety had been overwhelmed by passion and surrender.

Thus, instead of a map, he showed her the way to his bed where she soon exchanged her virginity for the essential qualification to travel to Chicago with him. A few minutes later she qualified again.

And she qualified anew each of the next three days when she would visit his hotel to secrete belongings from her room to take with her to Chicago. When her cache was adequate, she slipped out of her mother's big Victorian house in Rensburgh sometime in the wee hours of the morning and departed with a handsome traveling man on an eastbound train to span those thirty long miles that stood between listless Rensburgh and cosmopolitan Chicago.

She didn't say anything. Either her mother or brother,

Otis, would talk her out of it, she knew. But they didn't understand. She just left a note:

"Dear Mother: Please do not worry about me. I have a rare chance to check out opportunities beyond Rensburgh, including Chicago. It may be the chance of a lifetime. It came up suddenly and I had to take it. I'll let you know when I am settled. Love, Emily."

"I'll get the railroad detectives on it right away," roared brother Otis the instant his weeping mother read the note to him.

Otis P. Hampton was the assistant vice president of the Great Lakes Pacific Railroad. A local boy, he was making it big with the railroad. If he played company politics right, "assistant" would soon be removed from his title. He would be a vice president and who knows whether in time the word "vice" could also be erased.

But right now there was a young sister to worry about, a sister dizzy with wild fantasies of Chicago. He was pretty sure he knew what lured her away. But he didn't know which traveling man it might be. The detectives could find her, though. And also find him. And when they did, he would wish he had never dishonored the sister of an assistant vice president of the Great Lakes Pacific Railroad.

"No, dear," pleaded his mother. "No detectives. It's bad enough as it is. But we don't want the whole town knowing detectives are searching for my runaway girl.

"Besides, she'll come back."

And she did. About two months later. In tears and shame.

"I've been such a fool," she bawled as soon as she could let herself go in the comfort of home with her mother beside her and her brother quickly on the scene from GLP headquarters.

"Who made the fool of you," demanded Otis.

"Emory Pastwell," she sobbed. "He seemed so handsome and nice. And then I told him about the baby."

"Baby?" her mother was incredulous.

"And I thought he'd be happy and we'd get married."

"You're preg...," gasped Otis, quickly catching himself before using the vulgarity in the presence of women. "You're with child?"

"Instead," she hesitated as her voice failed her, "he left."

"Left?"

"The next morning he was gone. No note. Just gone." And she broke into uncontrolled sobbing.

This time Otis didn't mention it to his mother. He raged straight to his office.

"Get me the detectives," he bellowed to his secretary as he stormed past her.

Within minutes, the chief of detectives for the Great Lakes Pacific Railroad stood at attention in the office of the assistant vice president and heard orders to find a traveling man named Pastwell and deliver him to the assistant vice president in person.

"I don't know how you'll do it. Just do it."

"That's our business, sir," said the chief. "We'll find him." And they did.

Less than a week later a dandy who had recently been well-dressed but now looked a bit the worse for wear found himself scurrying into the office of the assistant vice president of the Great Lakes Pacific Railroad. He had no choice. A burly detective was on each side of him.

"Mr. Hampton wishes to see this gentleman," a detective instructed the secretary.

"Hampton," thought Emory G. Pastwell. The name sounded familiar. What was the last name of that naive Rensburgh girl who made the mistake of getting pregnant? Could this mean the kind of trouble he had never worried about with all the others he had loved and forgotten in the past?

And then he found himself rushing through the door. He brushed himself off, reaching for whatever dignity he could find between two burly detectives and sought to retrieve the practiced self-assurance that formed the tools of his trade.

"That'll be all for now, boys, if you wouldn't mind waiting outside," said the assistant vice president to the burly detectives.

"Sir, what is this all about?" The traveling man feigned indignation. A good offense might be the best defense. In fact, it might be the only defense.

With hard, cold, clipped diction, Otis P. Hampton responded:

"Mr. Pastwell, I've invited you here for the wedding."

"Wedding? What wedding?"

Hampton gripped the peddler with a vicious, unyielding stare, "Your wedding, Mr. Pastwell. Your wedding to my sister."

"But, I don't recall a betrothal…"

"Oh, there's a betrothal, all right. There's also a baby. And you are going to be a good husband and father. You are going to have a wedding, all right. And that's not all. You are also going to make my little sister happy. You are going to be kind and faithful to her and you are going to try very hard to make me like you and respect you as a brother-in-law."

Just as Emory was trying to think of a response that might open the way for some type of negotiations, Otis continued:

"And if you fail in any way at any time, it would give me great pleasure to so advise the railroad detectives, who would take delight in tracking you down and seeing to it that you disappear from the face of the earth."

Enough. "Now, see here. You can't threaten me like that."

"Mr. Pastwell, that is not a threat. That is a solemn promise. Do one thing to disappoint me and you will not be seen or heard from again.

"Now let us get over to your prospective bride who awaits with your prospective child and make final arrangements for tonight's nuptials."

"Tonight's?"

He was trapped. He couldn't break and run. There was no place to run to. He might as well have been in prison.

Emory Pastwell gulped nervously when he said, "I do." But he got the words out in the Hampton home that evening.

Thus did the happy couple begin their blissful life together. Indeed, the frustration felt by the beaming groom did not show on the surface. He was a most attentive husband to his wife who was bearing his child. He had tangled once with the Great Lakes Pacific Railroad detectives and he did not want to again. Moreover, he had no doubt of the will of his brother-in-law, the assistant vice president. His life was too precious to him to challenge such a credible authority.

There was only one problem. How could he support a family? He had never been a very successful peddler, at least not in peddling his wares. Much better at peddling wild oats. But now he needed dependable income.

Interestingly, one brother-in-law with connections in high places had already thought of that. He had assumed that Emory G. Pastwell was more wind than sales, but he had thought of a way to make use of whatever vending talents the man had so that even so sorry a specimen would be a good provider for his little sister.

He summoned his once-reluctant brother-in-law to his office at the Great Lakes Pacific headquarters.

"Emory," he said, "I know you have had your own career. But in case you would like a slight change, one that would still involve your talents as a salesman, I wonder if you would undertake a special project for me."

Emory would be pleased to tackle anything that might make money and satisfy his brother-in-law.

"I would be most interested in doing whatever I can to help," he said.

"Great. Tell ya what I have in mind. The need for new towns to be developed in the Western Frontier becomes more apparent every day. Homesteading has produced denser settlement and with more people comes the opportunity for more business. New towns should spring up along the railroad, almost everywhere we install a fuel stop."

"Yes, but how can a salesman do anything about that?"

"Let me get to that. I am sure a grateful railroad would donate land for a town site to someone it could count on to build a town where it would serve the railroad's purpose."

"You mean, and I could sell off the lots or develop them?" The picture was getting clearer to Emory Pastwell and he liked what he saw. It looked like piles of money.

"Exactly. Just so you keep the railroad's counsel so that both your and our interests would coincide."

"Of course. But where…"

Otis Hampton opened a huge map of the land through which the Great Lakes Pacific Railroad ran. He spread it out on a large table along the wall near his desk, giving both men the opportunity to study it.

"There are lots of opportunities. But one of the brighter ones, I think, occurs near a tiny town called Sierra Mesa. Right there." He pointed to a speck on the map.

"From the complaints I see regularly, many new businessmen are not at all pleased with the town as it exists. I believe there is a fine opportunity, indeed a need, to develop a new town next to it to replace it. And this time to lay it out in a sensible manner. In other words, to see what is wrong with Sierra Mesa and do it right this time."

Emory G. Pastwell's eyes brightened. Here was a chance to make money. Here was a chance to get away, for a while at least, from the stranglehold of marriage.

And, most important, perhaps, here was a chance to please a temperamental and powerful brother-in-law. Why, Otis P. Hampton may be one of the few assistant vice presidents of a railroad who did not have a town named after him.

Emory G. Pastwell would take care of that. Whatever else there was about the town site, the name would be Hampton City.

THREE

When Emory G. Pastwell returned to Sierra Mesa via the westbound Great Lakes Pacific train, he was every bit the show-horse dandy he had been on his initial arrival. He was a spectacle then; entertaining, different. Now he was wearing rather thin. We may have been a bunch of hicks far out here in the country, a long way from the sophisticated ways of a city. But even to us it was apparent that he was trying too hard to have his clothing make his statement for him. Through the tall top hat and the long gray coat and the watch chain, accented by the ever-present cigar, he was determined to define himself as something special, set apart from and above the local gentry. Well, we gentry were perfectly happy to be set apart, but we weren't so sure who was above or below.

Some of the mystery was clearing up. He was no longer

empty handed, as he had been on his first visit. In the more appropriate manner of a salesman, this time he came bearing something. It looked like a simple map. He called it a plat.

It was all marked out in neat, straight lines. Some had names like Iowa and Indiana, or Elm and Main, designating them as streets. Others were oblongs with circled numbers in the middle, indicating they were lots to build upon. In the very center was a square that was to be the heart of Hampton City. Across the street on one side was the train station.

The Great Lakes Pacific Railroad obviously was to have a prominent place in Hampton City. There was to be no right side or wrong side of the tracks. The railroad would run through the core and unite rather than divide the community.

Indeed, Hampton City was to be built around the GLP's first fuel drop west of Sierra Mesa, just eleven miles away. And that fact sent the jitters through the old and established merchants of Sierra Mesa right away. They were getting along okay, but they certainly didn't need another town to compete with them right in the heart of their trading territory.

Becky and I indulged ourselves a twinge of superiority. Now we understood what we were watching from our hiding place in the old cellar as the dude from the East looked around the fuel drop. We were in on something long before others around Sierra Mesa knew anything was going on. It hardly mattered that we didn't know what we were in on at the time; we were in on it nevertheless.

But now we knew. The traveling man from the East had a town site in his possession, courtesy of the Great Lakes Pacific Railroad. He was more than the usual salesman or the normal businessman, but a lot of both. Starting a new town from scratch was a long cut above anything we had encountered before.

When Pastwell started passing out handbills about a meeting in the depot Thursday night after supper, the merchants were quick to clear their schedules to attend. And they urged their customers and everybody they ran into to be there, too. Safety in numbers, they figured, while they got a picture of what Pastwell had in mind for their community.

The word got all the way to the county seat in Gortonville and some Jefferson County officials were among those who responded to the handbill that proclaimed:

NEW TOWN
Learn all about exciting opportunities in Hampton City. The chance of a lifetime.
Pass it up and you will regret it the rest of your life.
Thursday, May 19, seven o'clock in the evening sharp.
Come to the Great Lakes Pacific Depot in Sierra Mesa to learn how you can get in on the ground floor. You will be creating a new city to serve the good people of western Jefferson County.

It wouldn't be right to say that the little train station was packed. Or that there was a standing-room crowd. No, that wouldn't do justice to the interest Pastwell had drummed up. Not everybody could even get in the building, but overflowed to the boardwalk outside.

Emory G. Pastwell had rigged up a little platform that set him a notch above the assembled crowd. "Boys," he declared to open his proceedings. Several of the bolder ladies of the community were there, too. But his introductory remark excluded them. He was talking only to the good, old boys of Jefferson County, east and west, Gortonville and Sierra Mesa, and everyone in-between and beyond.

And it wasn't long before the merchants of Sierra Mesa began to get the message. They didn't care much for what they heard.

"Hampton City is going to be the key city of this whole part of the state. Make no mistake about that. It will be, because it's going to be done right from the very beginning.

"The Great Lakes Pacific Railroad is solidly behind it. Fact is, the railroad is already putting out notices for businesses to be among the first to locate there. I've already received quite a bit of interest.

"Those who get in on the ground floor will get their building lots for both businesses and homes for half price. That's what I'm offering you tonight. Half price. You'll never have a chance like that again. Only you can't wait. You have to act now.

"I urgently encourage all of you living and working in Sierra Mesa to consider most seriously the opportunities awaiting you in Hampton City. Act now, gentlemen, or I'm afraid you may be stuck with worthless property here.

"Now I don't mean to take anything away from Sierra Mesa. A charming village. But it obviously was built to be temporary and with the coming of Hampton City its usefulness is about over.

"I urge you to think about it. Then act. Now."

Pastwell was as good as his word that he would stick around until all questions were answered and all orders taken for building lots. There were far more questions than sales.

Q. "Why close down Sierra Mesa? Why not have two towns."

A. "There isn't room for two towns. The Great Lakes Pacific Railroad has vast experience in these matters and assures me only one town can survive."

Q. "Why not let that be Sierra Mesa? Why start a new town when we already have one?"

A. "Because Sierra Mesa is a mess. It just doesn't work. It was never planned as a town. Hampton City will be done right from the start and will really amount to something. Sierra Mesa never could. The railroad knows that Sierra Mesa, far from promoting a new day, stands in the way of progress."

Q. "What gives you the right to start a new town?"

A. "I have considerable experience in organizing new ventures. The Great Lakes Pacific has full confidence in me. Why else do you think the railroad would entrust me with a town site from which it expects great things?"

Q. "Could I trade my Sierra Mesa property for a lot in Hampton City?"

A. "I would like to say yes. But I'm afraid not. Property in Sierra Mesa, I regret, is losing its value."

Q. "How would I know I am getting anything of value in Hampton City? It's a town that doesn't even exist."

A. "Ah, my friend, but it will. It will amount to far more

than Sierra Mesa ever could, because it will be well-planned and backed by the Great Lakes Pacific Railroad. You invest now at low prices and you will pride yourself in your wise choice for the rest of your life."

And so it went.

Some people in the crowd were stunned. Some were excited. Some were amused. But not many were fooled by his half-price bargain. Half price of what? He was setting the price and he could set it anywhere he thought would sell. Half price was just a gimmick.

Regardless of the slow sales on his opening offer, Pastwell was satisfied that his project was launched successfully.

Of all the people assembled that night, he was particularly intrigued by S. Franklin Pierce. Or, S. Franklin Pierce was intrigued by him. They couldn't help but be. Each might as well have found the twin brother he never knew he had.

A couple of county commissioners, the sheriff and the auditor all came over from Gortonville, and with them came state representative S. Franklin Pierce. He wasn't actually related to the fourteenth president, but concluded that use of the middle name would make it appear that he was. Besides, it gave him stature and an unforgettable aura. Plain old Sam Pierce wouldn't attract much attention. Or even Samuel F. Pierce. But S. Franklin Pierce, now there was a name that would register on folks when they got in the voting booth.

While the merchants parleyed elsewhere to ponder whether to ignore the challenge, fight back, or give in, Emory G. Pastwell and S. Franklin Pierce busied themselves treating, toasting and testing each other over get-acquainted drinks at the bar in the hotel.

"Well, Mr. Pastwell, now that you are engaged in building a city in our county, I trust you are now a legal resident of Jefferson County and therefore registered to vote."

"Not yet, but I just arrived. I fully intend to participate in all the affairs of the community. I view voting as a sacred duty."

"Good. Good," said Pierce. "I don't know what your politics may be, but I pride myself in being a judge of character and I believe you would be comfortable in the party with the future in this state. That's the Republican Party, of course."

Pastwell had never voted in his life. He had never thought about what he might possibly believe in politically. So he was certainly open to any offers, just as long as his powerful brother-in-law, the assistant vice president of the GLP, didn't mind.

Without letting on to the quality of his commitment to his sacred duty, he managed to get a general civics lesson right there in the bar. His companion expansively volunteered where to register to vote, how to register, where to vote and not so incidentally whom to vote for.

For S. Franklin Pierce was up for re-election, as a representative must be every other year. It was, regrettably, too late for Pastwell to register for the primary election, this new-fangled political contraption a new state was experimenting with because an ignorant electorate favored it. The voters seemed to think they could cut the power of party bosses by nominating party candidates through an election. It was almost un-American. But there was nothing Pierce and his ilk could do about it. The people had planted the primary in their constitution.

But he could forget the primary for now. The new voter could be eligible for the general election, and that's what really counted. Pierce faced no opponent in the primary election, but he would certainly have a contest in November and Mr. Pastwell's help would be most thoroughly appreciated.

His help most assuredly would include the vote. That, however, would be merely the beginning. This stranger, obviously a man of means, would do more than make a scratch in the voting booth. He would surely dig into his bank account.

It was time for the overture.

"Indeed, we can help each other, you and I," Pierce offered. "You support my re-election and I'm sure I can help give your town a little boost. All on the up and up, you understand."

And understand, Emory Pastwell certainly did. A little mutual back-scratching had always been his style.

"I believe we have business we can attend to, Mr. Pierce. Bartender, set 'em up again for a toast to our shared interests."

They drank to re-elections and new cities and departed for the evening, each confident he had made a valuable ally who could be used effectively in the coming trials of voters and investors.

The brother-in-law was true to his word. The railroad took firm first steps to bolster Hampton City's success. Otis P. Hampton, the assistant vice president, acted decisively to assure his sister Emily's well-being.

He assumed quite understandably that her husband was a no-account. So the only thing he could do was to use the railroad's power to give Emory Pastwell a deal he couldn't foul up. Make him rich and Emily and her expected child would likewise be rich.

Almost immediately the GLP started building its station. If not a Taj Mahal, the depot clearly was a full cut above the one in Sierra Mesa. It was a lot of station for a nonexistent town. Indeed, it would have complemented many a thriving community very nicely.

But even more important than the depot was the nearby hotel also being built by the railroad. Now, that was an open symbol of confidence. It told the world the Great Lakes Pacific Railroad was solidly behind this city. It also offered an additional advantage. Prospects lured to Hampton City in quest of opportunity could look the place over while tended to with all of the amenities of modern life even out here on the recent frontier.

And it sent the intended message to Sierra Mesa. We're bypassing you. You no longer count. Either join us or get out of our way.

Prospects did come. They also bought. The railroad's advertising campaign had been effective. Hampton City had secured its first store, which sent shock waves through both general stores of Sierra Mesa. Backed by the railroad, a bank opened.

But the going was slow, much slower than Emory Pastwell had expected. The fact was, he was struggling to maintain his false front of unparalleled prosperity on the meager earnings from early sales.

Most disappointing of all was Sierra Mesa. Some people,

mostly newcomers, still grumbled about the hodgepodge town that grew up helter-skelter in frontier days. But they didn't close their businesses and open new ones eleven miles away. They didn't board up their houses and pack off their households to new homes in Hampton City.

Sierra Mesa stayed pretty much as it was. Hampton City had a new railroad station and hotel, a few homes and a handful of businesses, but it had not taken off the way either Pastwell, his well-placed brother-in-law, or the railroad had envisioned.

They had done everything right. The Great Lakes Pacific had advertised opportunities far and wide. Pastwell had followed through with his sales pitch. He had attracted the attention of all the right people, threatened Sierra Mesa, appealed to greed in Gortonville and invested railroad money as his own to show confidence in the place.

In spite of it all, far from booming the way past experience dictated that it should, Hampton City was struggling.

There had to be a gimmick. There had to be. In the world of sales, there was always something that would make the sale. The longer Hampton City stagnated, the less confidence investors would have and the harder the sale would be. That's what happened when momentum was lost. Pastwell looked for a way to create a rush, a bandwagon, even a panic. Act now, the message had to be; wait at your own risk. There had to be something to put a threat behind the risk for those who waited—something and soon.

Representative S. Franklin Pierce stepped off the westbound GLP train from Gortonville. He checked into the hotel. It was time to put the bite on his new friend, Emory G. Pastwell, for a generous contribution to his re-election campaign.

His top hat occupying the neighboring chair at the table where Pastwell sat in the newly opened saloon, the dandy took in the Pierce arrival nonchalantly. He enjoyed the representative's company. It would be good to see him again. But there were other things, worrisome things, on a crowded mind right now.

But Emory Pastwell nonetheless managed to put on the

promoter's face, brimming with joy and confidence, to greet the state representative as he strolled into the saloon from the nearby hotel.

"Welcome. Welcome, my friend," enthused the salesman. "Here, let me buy you one. Tell me, what do you think of our thriving metropolis?"

"Well, it is good to be here, to see you again. But to tell you the truth, Emory, I thought there might be a bit more to Hampton City by now."

"Oh, a lot's in the works, Franklin. You know how these things go. Can't build everything all at once. Gets frustrating at times. But actually we're well ahead of schedule."

"Sure you are," thought S. Franklin Pierce. But he said nothing to dampen the optimism.

"Mighty good to hear, Emory," he said. "This country needs Hampton City. This county needs Hampton City. This state needs Hampton City. I'll do anything I can to help it succeed."

"Why, thank you, Franklin. Appreciate your support. You'll be mighty proud of what we have here in a couple of years."

Pierce nodded as he sipped from his glass. It was time to get down to cases.

"Good." He let his eyes drop, interlocked his fingers on the table in front of him, then with practiced understatement of the urgency of his predicament, he said somberly, "Emory, I need your help. I have a re-election fight on my hands and I need to finance a campaign. With all of your resources, how much can I count on from you? Maybe a hundred dollars?"

Somehow Emory Pastwell managed to avoid choking on the sip of whiskey he had just taken. A hundred dollars? Where would he come up with a sum like that and for what purpose?

But he managed to maintain the countenance of confidence. "Whatever it takes, Franklin. But what's the worry? What problem could you possibly have in this election? Isn't your re-election assured?"

"Far from it," Pierce advised, donning an expression of earnest concern. "I'm in a real dog fight. I have an opponent who's running on a platform of carving off a chunk of

Jefferson County on the east and joining it with a chunk of Davis County to form a new county."

A new county? Suddenly Partwell was all ears. The gimmick may have just been delivered by Representative S. Franklin Pierce.

"Can you do that? Form a new county, I mean?"

"Of course. It happens every session. One of the main things the legislature does is consider adjusting county lines because of the new growth and population shifts from homesteading."

"But you don't want this county?"

"It's not really up to me," Pierce emphasized, hoping to make the point that he was merely the servant of the people tending to their business as they wanted him to. Yet, since he also sought to present a front of principle and independent thinking, he went on, "But, no, not really. It doesn't make much sense. That's not really an area of new growth. It's just a bunch of folks disgruntled with Gortonville who think they can get a better deal.

"You know the area. Heavily settled by folks from the South after the Civil War. They think they'd really be creating something of their own if they took part of Jefferson County, part of Davis County and made Jefferson Davis County out of it."

"Doesn't sound very patriotic to me. Almost treason, I'd say. Aren't most people against it? Why is it a threat to your re-election?"

"The folks in Gortonville are opposed. But lots of people to the east are in favor of it. All the southerners. Some of the rest, too, mainly because Gortonville is opposed. You know how these local spats shape up. If the town's for something, the country folk are against it. And the other way around."

"Why don't you just stay out of it?"

"Can't. It wouldn't be the appropriate thing to do. A public official has to take a stand. It's a matter of principle. Besides I promised the merchants of Gortonville when they put up money for my campaign."

"Oh," said Emory Pastwell. "So that's the way it works," thought Emory Pastwell.

"But they didn't put up enough money to pay for your campaign?" he asked.

"Oh, they were generous to a fault," Pierce replied. "But it takes a lot to run an effective campaign."

He didn't add, "Especially if you want to have something left over for yourself."

"I think I could come up with the hundred," Pastwell said. "But there is an issue I would like to talk to you about."

Franklin Pierce was prepared for it. That's the way the system worked. "Shoot," he said.

"Jefferson Davis County on the east doesn't make sense," said Pastwell. "But how about a new county on the west? This whole area west of the Hunkapapa River is cut off from the rest of Jefferson County. It's a long way from Gortonville. It's set off by itself so much it's known more as the Hunkapapa District than a part of Jefferson County. It's had quite a bit of growth since homesteading. Seems to me a new county, maybe Hampton County, would make sense. With Hampton City as county seat, of course."

Pierce sat back, pondering. He didn't need a county on the west as well as one on the east to get mixed up in his re-election campaign.

"You make a good point," he said. "But let's not let it get all tangled up with politics in this campaign. Why don't we wait until after the election to think it through. Counties ought to be above politics."

One of the most political things a politician does is to declare a political issue to be above politics, but that was fine with Emory G. Pastwell. He had broken through. He had his gimmick: A new county formed right around Hampton City with a courthouse in the Hampton City square.

As soon as he got the word to his brother-in-law, he would have the hundred dollars needed to grease the corridors of the Capitol when the legislature started to roll.

Hampton County, here we come!

FOUR

Otis P. Hampton was relieved. At last there was the chance for real movement on Hampton City. A hundred dollars was easy for a helpful politician who was well-placed. Many politicians cost much more than that.

Indeed, double the amount would make sense. Give the pol one hundred dollars for his campaign; then, assuming he wins, give him another one hundred dollars to cover his imaginary debt. If he doesn't win, switch the second hundred to the victor to begin currying favor.

Hampton County, um. Had a nice ring to it. It was appropriate to have Hampton City, especially if it became the regional center of its promise. But it was no more than simply appropriate. After all, many assistant vice presidents of railroads all over the country had towns named after them.

But a county and a town! No one he could think of had that distinction. Surely, the double honor would distinguish him from the run-of-the-mill assistant vice presidents and help to get the modifier "assistant" erased from the nameplate on his door.

Hampton had to hand it to his brother-in-law. He wouldn't have believed that Emory G. Pastwell possessed the gumption to come up with an idea like creating a county and following through with the political moxie to make it a real possibility.

The assistant vice president had been frustrated by the slow pace of Hampton City. It should have been a sure winner. The railroad had followed proven procedure in creating a new town and getting a tired, old hamlet out of the way of progress. The Great Lakes Pacific Railroad had an established track record in this regard. Many a tumble-down old village had been swept into the dustbin of history to make way for a modern town that fit the railroad's purposes.

He attributed the disappointing development to the ineptitude of his sister's shotgun husband. But the possibility of Hampton County more than offset his chagrin.

"Proceed with the one hundred dollars immediately," his note to his brother-in-law directed, with two hundred dollars enclosed. "Then add one hundred dollars right after the election. The stated purpose will be to pay off the campaign debt that you suppose exists. There won't be a debt, of course, but you can pretend. That's the way politics works. Give it to him with an appropriate reminder of the need for his support for a new county. Remind him, naturally, that the county makes sense and merely requires his good judgment. Let him think that you believe the money you have given him has nothing to do with it.

"If the other fellow should happen to win, give the second one hundred dollars to him and start building bridges."

With cash and instructions in hand, Emory G. Pastwell headed straight for Gortonville and the law office of State Representative S. Franklin Pierce. As the train rumbled across the bridge over the Hunkapapa River, he was struck by the change in the landscape from the western part of Jefferson County to the eastern region.

He also took note of the amount of time required to reach the county seat from the west end. He concluded his county not only could be a reality, but should be. It was more than a sales gimmick; it made sense. It surprised him to be seized by such a notion, for it really didn't matter how much sense it made. He was just looking for something to close a deal.

Representative Pierce was of course deeply grateful for the generous campaign contribution.

"Emory, my friend, this donation just may be what saves me in this election," he told his collaborator. "It's a tough race, but this comes in just the nick of time to turn my campaign around."

"Franklin, I can't tell you what a pleasure it gives me to be in a position to contribute to the cause of good government," Pastwell replied.

"I need hardly add," he added, "what an honor it shall be for me to cast my first vote in this state for so distinguished a state representative who it shall be my privilege to support for higher office hereafter."

Pierce planted a firm hand on his supporter's shoulder. "I hope never to disappoint you," he said with an expression of resolve.

An unintended double meaning occurred to Pastwell. He suspected that a politician seldom disappoints large contributors. But he said nothing more. He certainly would not be disappointed if his prominent ally managed to acquire a county for him.

In the weeks leading up to the election, Pastwell saw Pierce only a couple of times, but the occasions didn't lend themselves to business. Pierce came to Sierra Mesa and Hampton City to give speeches and shake hands. Mostly, though, he stayed on the east side where most of the voters resided.

As the campaign wound down to election day, the polls were a bit of a concern for Pastwell. Since he had never voted before, he was unsure of the procedure. Yet his pretense dictated that he dare not show his confusion. Even so minor a distraction might unmask the character of confidence and prosperity he presented to the people of the Hunkapapa District of western Jefferson County.

For a time he contemplated missing the event by being in Rensburgh on election day. His expectant wife would provide the perfect excuse. He would have to be on hand for the arrival of his first born. Everyone could understand why he could not miss so important an event.

But the baby wasn't due that soon. Later in November would be more like it. Besides, he had made such an issue out of supporting Representative Pierce that he could not afford to risk losing expensive influence by missing an election. He vaguely was aware of absentee ballots, but trying to figure out that procedure would simply add to his dilemma.

One development that gave him a sense of comfort was the new voting precinct located in the Great Lakes Pacific station. The railroad had made it available to the Jefferson County clerk so that residents in and around Hampton City would not have to go to Sierra Mesa to cast their ballots. The station was practically home to Emory Pastwell, which helped to overcome election-day jitters.

On election day, Pastwell watched earnestly, albeit cautiously, while openly focusing attention on his cigar as others marched up to the polling place set up in the GLP depot. He noted how they signed the poll book, took a ballot and disappeared behind a curtain enclosing a small cell. A long minute later they emerged with satisfied expressions on their faces, marched back to the table where the election board sat stone-faced, and deposited the folded ballot through a slot in a box.

The process looked easy enough. He could do that. And he did. He found voting was no problem. It was easy. What wasn't easy was figuring out all of those names along side offices he had never heard of. What was a county auditor, for heaven's sake? Even more baffling were all those arcane questions.

Candidates were bad enough, but at least they were people. Emory Pastwell did not know about ballot measures on which he apparently was expected to vote yes or no. What was that large amount of money for a high school all about?

Why did these yokels on the frontier need a high school anyway? Or what was that thing about whether the land commissioner should be elected or appointed by the governor? What was a land commissioner anyway?

Prior to meeting Representative Pierce, about the only politician Pastwell recognized was William McKinley. He searched the ballot high and low for president of the United States, but to no avail. Nothing informed him that McKinley had two more years in office before his name would appear on the ballot again. And then it would appear only to the extent that it would be linked to the electors who would actually choose the president in Electoral College.

Pastwell did not tarry long with either the ballot measures or his perplexity over the missing presidency. Too much time spent in the voting booth would draw suspicion.

In the end he voted for just one spot on the ballot. He scrawled an X in the box beside the name of S. Franklin Pierce. He carefully folded his ballot the way others had, marched matter-of-factly to the box with the slot and dropped the completed ballot in. Then he turned like a man with more important missions to attend to and marched out of the depot, leaving a cloud of cigar smoke as a symbol of self-importance in his wake.

Of course S. Franklin Pierce did not lose. There never had been a contest, although he managed to spook the merchants of Gortonville and a few others into thinking there was. The other fellow, a southerner, ran like a pre-Civil War Southern candidate, courtly, proper, warning constantly against loss of local control to central authority.

His platform, however, was heavy with Civil War symbolism. He ran almost exclusively on a pledge to carve Jefferson Davis County out of Jefferson and Davis counties. He picked up the Dixie vote. It was a solid bloc, but only made up about a fourth of the electorate. It had been a big enough bloc to win him the Democratic nomination in the primary. But most of the other Democrats, Populists and Independents were too suspicious of a Confederate to vote for him.

Thus, the rest of the district went almost as solidly for

Pierce, even on the west end where strong misgivings about the representative were overshadowed by distrust of a Dixie candidate. So State Representative S. Franklin Pierce had his re-election by nearly a three to one margin.

The money from the Great Lakes Pacific Railroad via Emory G. Pastwell and that from the merchants of Gortonville had very little to do with it. It would have been impossible to invent ways to spend all of their contributions on a campaign. Some handbills, a few posters, and ads in the local weekly newspapers simply did not cost that much. No candidate for the legislature since statehood, and most assuredly not in territorial days, had ever squandered such a large sum as one hundred dollars on a campaign.

Neither did S. Franklin Pierce. So here he was with a small fortune of more than one thousand dollars on hand for his personal use. Properly invested, it might make him rich with either property or power or both.

So he was not expecting additional largesse, but was no less grateful when his friend, Emory G. Pastwell, the wealthy man from Chicago with ties to the Great Lakes Pacific Railroad and a town site of his own, popped off the eastbound train in Gortonville once more and made his way to Pierce's law office.

"What a surprise, Emory," said the newly re-elected state representative over his outstretched hand. "To what do I owe the pleasure?"

Pastwell returned the greetings. "Always my pleasure, Franklin," he said as he gripped the legislator's hand. Then he stretched out his hand again, this time with an envelope in it.

"Congratulations on an impressive victory," he said. "Just a little something to help cover any left-over campaign bills after such a strenuous race. That ought to let you get down to business without having financial worries to think about."

Pierce was astonished, but was too experienced in the art of political take to appear dumbfounded. Ten crisp ten dollar bills. An additional one hundred dollars to add to his bonanza.

"You know a lot more about the rigors of politics than you

let on, my friend," oozed the state representative. "I've been wondering how I would ever get out from under the burden of debt. Public service makes such demands on those of us who are willing to give of ourselves. But your thoughtfulness and generosity will help mightily. I thank you. I thank you not only for the money, but also for the thoughtfulness."

"My privilege and pleasure," responded Pastwell, equally keeping a straight face.

It was time to make the move.

"I hate to bring business up at a time like this with the election just over," Pastwell declared, obviously eager to do exactly that, "but I wonder while I'm here if we could discuss one little matter that I briefly alluded to before the election. It is rather important."

S. Franklin Pierce remembered. Hampton County. He wasn't enthusiastic about it. After all, he represented Jefferson County, so it was hardly in his interest to carve up his own county.

The threat of Jefferson Davis County on the east evaporated with the election. Now here was Hampton County beyond the Hunkapapa River on the west.

True, county lines changed every time the legislature met. Population kept growing and shifting so naturally counties had to grow and shift, too, to reflect the changes. But normally legislators were not expected to support moves to divide their own counties. Others would take care of the issue, allowing them just to vote no.

"Well, I'm always ready to do business," replied Representative Pierce. "That's what I'm here for. Is it about that county you were talking about?"

"That's it," replied Emory Pastwell, pleased that the idea had not been lost in the hectic activity of electioneering. "You remember we were going to leave it until after the election so's it wouldn't get messed up with politics. Now that the election's over, it's probably time to get ready, however you do that, to take it up at the legislature."

Pierce couldn't duck, not with two hundred dollars in his cache and a valuable friendship that could be worth much more than that if he used Pastwell right. But what would he lose among his supporters here in Gortonville if he became the advocate for the Hunkapapa District to break away?

"It's tough business," said the representative grimly. "Takes a lot of time and effort. First you have to get support from the rest of the county, like the merchants in Gortonville. They are usually skeptical about changing county lines.

"Then you have to get a bill drawn up. Fortunately, with my legal training, I'm better than most at that, but it does take time to get it right. Then you have to start selling the idea to the rest of the legislature so they don't feel surprised when they arrive for the session. All in all, it's a costly and time-consuming proposition."

"Be glad to help however I can," said Pastwell. "I think the Hunkapapa District would make an ideal county by itself. Hampton County. Every time I cross the bridge on the train I realize the difference and the time it takes to travel to Gortonville. The people and the state would be well served."

"Your offer of help is welcome, Emory, and I may need to call on you. Trouble is, most of the work has to be done by the legislator himself."

And then another diabolical thought entered the avaricious mind of S. Franklin Pierce.

"You were so thoughtful and generous to come with your gift today," he said. "The problem is, that covers about half of my debt, but there's the other half I have to attend to. I'm afraid that may take so much of my time that I couldn't do justice to your plan for a new county."

Pastwell was beginning to understand politics. "But suppose I could come up with a few dollars more, say another hundred. Would that give you time to work on Hampton County?" he inquired.

The picture was getting clearer all the time. He was starting to appreciate his brother-in-law's knowledge of politics. No wonder Otis Hampton had volunteered the second one hundred dollars.

"Oh, you shouldn't do that, Emory," said a crafty Pierce. "You've done more than enough already. 'Course a hundred dollars would free me up to devote most of my time between now and the session to preparing your legislation."

"Then it's the least I can do," said Emory Pastwell as he contemplated in his own mind whether he could scrape up one hundred dollars right away without having to send for it to his brother-in-law in Rensburgh and wait for the reply.

"You devote your time to the common good. I can at least help to free you from the confines of campaign costs to do your public service," Pastwell said as an idea was starting to form on how he could come up with the extra one hundred dollars.

For the sake of family tranquillity, he was going to have to put in an appearance in Rensburgh. He could surely explain satisfactorily the investment of an extra hundred while there.

"I must go home for a few days," he explained. "My wife, you know, is about to present me with my first child. I must be on hand for the blessed event."

"Why, by all means," a beaming Representative Pierce assured him. "You must be at your wife's bedside at a time like this."

"When I get back I'll stop by with the money to wipe out what is left of your campaign debt. You can count on it."

"Thank you, Emory. I shall count on it. And I will get started on Hampton County while you are away. You can count on that."

The westbound train returned him to Hampton City to pack his bags and be ready to board the eastbound train the following morning.

Pastwell had no doubt that his brother-in-law would come up with the money. That was not what occupied his mind as the passing scene shifted from the wide open spaces of the range around Sierra Mesa to a mix of range and large farms and homesteads around Gortonville. From there on, there was a gradual but steady diminishing of farm size as the Great Lakes Pacific train rumbled eastward.

On the second day of his journey it struck him funny how the towns tended to grow in size while the farms got smaller as the train made its way easterly. The range was gone. Stubble from the harvest of small grain was mainly behind him. More and more he stared at the remains of cornfields as he sped along. The thought, however, was but a brief respite in his brooding about another matter as the rails stretched endlessly over the many miles to Rensburgh.

Sooner or later, he supposed, he would have to settle down with his wife and child to form a home. It was nothing he had ever planned to do and he was not looking forward to it. But even more unnerving was the thought that it would become necessary for him to live permanently in Hampton City. Rensburgh would be bad enough. Even Chicago. But being married and a family man in a town like Hampton City. How frightfully confining.

That decision, however, would be faced later as he forced the problem from his mind when the big train steamed into the flagship station at Rensburgh. His facade was all confidence and joy as he arrived at the Victorian house that was the Hampton family home, in time to be with his wife while his little daughter was born.

He had not seen his lovely wife for these many months he had been out West. He was amazed at how grotesque her body had become. But he refrained from showing his disappointment as he embraced her warmly, if cautiously, and kissed her firmly enough to give a display of passion.

"Emory, darling, you've been away so long," Emily scolded. "I could hardly stand it."

"Far too long, my love. Far too long," he replied and outwardly looked as though he meant it. "But it is for a good cause. Soon you, I and our baby will have a home that does justice to a wife like you."

"But we can have a home right here. My mother would love it. She adores you, you know."

Adores? Well, that would have come as a surprise to Mrs. Hampton, although she would willingly tolerate her son-in-law to have her daughter and grandchild under her roof and care. Fortunately, Pastwell thought, that would be impossible.

Life under the roof of his mother-in-law would be even worse than a home in Hampton City.

"That would be most welcome," he said. "I regret, though, that my venture would require that we make our home in Hampton City. I assure you, you'll love it there."

Emily had never satisfied her taste for Chicago. Hampton City would put her so far out in the sticks she might never see civilization again.

But every time the subject came up, her brother agreed with her husband. He insisted even over his mother's protests, "Emory is absolutely right. He is the founder of a town. He cannot expect others to have confidence in Hampton City if he does not show enough confidence in it to make his home there, too."

Emily, whose tastes for the big city were paramount in her mind, was not surrendering easily to life on the frontier. But during one of their discussions she was distracted from her argument by pains such as she had never before experienced. Labor pains. The baby was due.

The doctor was urgently sent for and he was on his way. She would have to think of her responsibility to Hampton City later.

Meanwhile, the first squall from his first-born reaffirmed Emory G. Pastwell's fear of what a living hell family life would be.

Looking for every excuse to get out of the big Victorian house with the perpetual noise-maker inside, Pastwell found plenty of time to discuss strategy with his brother-in-law, who had no problem coming up with one hundred dollars more.

To Otis P. Hampton, three hundred dollars to buy a helpful politician was peanuts. The Great Lakes Pacific Railroad would not be where it was today without having ready cash like that on hand for political favors large and small.

And so, for an extra one hundred dollars, three hundred dollars in all, Hampton County was headed for the state legislature in January in the portfolio of newly re-elected Representative S. Franklin Pierce, who was already counting future dollars from his rich Chicago friend. They would help to move him up the ladder, first to the state Senate, then maybe governor or even United States senator.

"Be sure you are in the Capitol every day to guide our bill through to passage," Otis P. Hampton instructed his brother-in-law.

He sought to teach the art and science of lobbying to the man who was the father of his sister's child and the man in whom he had trusted a mission for his railroad. The assistant vice president of the GLP still had little faith in Emory Pastwell, but even such a specimen could hardly foul up the deal he was offering. And his brother-in-law did show some spirit and imagination in coming up with this county scheme.

After the crash course presented by his brother-in-law on political influence, Emory G. Pastwell was off on another long train ride to the West. This one eventually would take him all the way to the Capitol to join Representative Pierce. To gain passage of a bill to create Hampton County he would have to enter a complicated process of government he knew nothing about. But he could learn. After all, it was just part of a sales gimmick.

Whatever the mystery that lay in the Capitol, he was free again. At least temporarily. The few days spent with his wife and her family were even more disheartening than he had feared. After the baby was born, there was no rest or quiet day or night. How had he ever allowed himself to become a husband and father?

The Capitol and this new world he was entering would save him from those duties for the time being. He could devote his energies to Hampton County, which was now a long step closer to reality. With it would come the financial boom when Hampton City enjoyed untold growth.

FIVE

The Capitol was a strange and wary place for Emory G. Pastwell. When he walked into the rotunda and tasted the grandeur of this temple to democracy, he felt strangely small and insignificant.

His every intention was to present the aura of big and important; thus small and insignificant was hardly the introduction to the Capitol he sought as he strode under its dome for the first time. He had never visited a Capitol before, not even the one in Springfield.

He had been in Springfield several times, but going to the statehouse had not occurred to him.

Fortunately, he had a solid connection in Representative S. Franklin Pierce and the importance of the Pierce alliance grew on him as he gradually acquainted himself with the strange processes that unfolded underneath the dome. His friend and recipient of three hundred dollars of Great Lakes Pacific Railroad money was chosen assistant majority whip and, perhaps even more significant, chairman of the Committee on Community Governance.

He dare not let on that he had somewhat less than the vaguest idea what an assistant majority whip was. Nor that he was lost in the maze of the committee system that operated the legislature. But he came to realize that a chairman had certain perquisites not bestowed upon his colleagues in the general membership and that an assistant whip had something to do with lining up votes for the position of the majority caucus. And he had learned what a caucus was. At first he thought it was just a closed meeting. But he finally figured out that when members of one party met, excluding all others, they were holding a caucus.

S. Franklin Pierce was as good as his three-hundred-dollar word in positioning himself well to see the creation of Hampton County through the complex process of legislating. Not only would he preside over the committee that considered the legislation, but also his help would include the final act of nailing down the support of a friendly governor.

Pastwell was a bit surprised to discover that he was just one of many men who were not in the legislature, but nonetheless spent their days in the Capitol, hanging around the lobbies just outside the doors of both the House of Representatives and the Senate. His county mission was not going to be the lonely vigil that he had supposed it would be. It had never occurred to him that whole careers could be based on blocking or shaping the making of law, and affluent careers they were at that.

They all had things they wanted from the legislature, usually for companies they worked for or clients they served. Mostly they sought special treatment for business, or at least for certain businesses. For the most part, they wanted the legislature to prevent the law from meddling in the ways businesses reaped their profits, but they also sought particular laws that would give their companies a slight edge over their competitors.

"All I'm asking for is just a little unfair advantage," crowed James W. Keater, who lobbied for a group of independent banks. His big goal this session was to gain his clients freedom from regulation on real-estate loans that would not be granted state-chartered banks.

The most generous purveyor of favors of all the men who frequented the Capitol lobby by day and the Capital Hotel by night actually wanted nothing. But he wanted nothing very much.

He was Henry ("just call me Hank") Waddington, who represented the mining industry. He was there not to pass legislation, but to see that no legislation was passed affecting mining. Free-wheeling mine owners were happy with things just as they were. Their employees might not be, but they were not yet well enough organized to have their interests represented in the lobbies of the Capitol and the saloon of the Capital Hotel.

Emory G. Pastwell was soon at home. The process was confusing, but the procedure was familiar. It was just a case of sales. Legislators were the buyers and all you needed was the right gimmick.

He had been instructed by his brother-in-law, Otis P. Hampton, the assistant vice president of the Great Lakes Pacific Railroad, to keep an eye on railway legislation generally and to help the railroad lobbyist, Theodore H. Milton, in any way he could. His first duty remained to establish Hampton County and make Hampton City the county seat. But while he was at it he could guard against the state's interference with railroad business, unless that interference produced a little unfair advantage for the GLP.

If the process in the corridors of the Capitol was complex, the other one where the actual decisions were made was not. The saloon in the Capital Hotel was familiar territory to Emory Pastwell. The grand hotel was built not far from the Capitol by entrepreneurs who correctly saw state government as a growth industry. The biennial legislative session was pure gravy.

Pastwell stayed in the Capital Hotel. He first checked in just for convenience because of the hotel's proximity to the

Capitol. But he needed only one evening to realize that he had stumbled into the right decision. Nearly all of the legislators stayed there, too, as did the others who occupied the lobbies of the Capitol by day.

The saloon was the gathering place for nearly all at the end of the work day. Pastwell learned quickly that most legislators did not buy their own drinks and meals. Indeed, the gentlemen of the lobby often stumbled over one another in their zeal to pick up the tab.

More Great Lakes Pacific money was to be dedicated to a worthy cause.

> *BUY FOOD AND BOOZE STOP THAT'S WHAT YOU'RE SUPPOSED TO DO STOP.*

His brother-in-law had replied in a brusque telegram to Pastwell's hasty query about the big spending that was thrust upon him:

> *LEGISLATORS EXPECT FREE FOOD AND DRINK STOP BIG MONEY STOP WHAT SHOULD I DO STOP AWAIT INSTRUCTIONS STOP.*

"It's only fair," Representative Pierce explained. "After all, the legislators are here as a public duty. Their piddling remuneration does not begin to cover the costs of tending to the people's business. A bit of help with drink and food merely enables them to serve without the sacrifice being unduly burdensome."

Through the bar of the Capital Hotel and S. Franklin Pierce, Pastwell soon made the acquaintance of many other legislators. He had no trouble introducing the concept of Hampton County to them. Indeed, many seemed vaguely aware of it. Pierce, in return for three hundred dollars, had laid the groundwork before the session convened.

Pierce had drafted a bill. Soon he would be presiding over hearings on it in the committee that he chaired.

Pastwell had read it. Unfamiliar as he was with the

legalese of legislation he wasn't sure just what it said, and he could easily get lost in all the metes and bounds. The important point was what the legal mishmash really meant: It clearly designated Hampton County as the area of Jefferson County west of the Hunkapapa River. The bill also declared that Hampton City would be county seat.

But one thing bothered Pastwell. The bill called for elections in the regular election cycle the following year for the commission and a range of other county officers who would operate the new county. It would delay organizing Hampton County until then.

He did not want to wait that long to make Hampton City a county seat. Indeed, he might not be able to afford to wait so long.

Pastwell searched through the bewilderment of law books to see if the establishment of other counties would offer guidance. As best he could make out from digging through the state's code, laws varied substantially on the formation of new counties.

Most seemed to hold the elections the following year, as Pierce's bill did and that is when a new county would become officially organized. But some set up special elections within ninety days. Some had the governor declare a newly approved county to be organized with the appointment of a temporary county clerk to preside over county records until an election could be held.

That model appealed to Pastwell. Get the county officially in business and get on with selling the county seat. Why wait for elections?

But another thing also puzzled him. Nowhere could he find a law establishing a county that dictated where the county seat would be.

"That's right," said Representative Pierce. "Not one of 'em names the county seat. But that's no reason the next one can't."

"If the law doesn't make it clear, how do you determine a county seat?" Pastwell wanted to know.

"Wherever the records are kept and the commission sits. If a governor declares a new county organized before elections are held, he may designate a temporary seat. But why take chances? We spell it out in law and you don't have to worry about Sierra Mesa mistakenly being used."

Why, indeed. Pastwell appreciated that he had spent the Great Lakes Pacific money wisely in gaining the support and know-how of S. Franklin Pierce.

He broached the subject of a temporary clerk to be caretaker of county records until an election could be held, thus assuring the early creation of Hampton County and the expedient development of Hampton City in the process.

"Bring it up at the hearing," Pierce suggested. "You'll want to testify anyway. Ask for an amendment."

"Why don't we just fix it in advance?"

"Nah. We have to save something for the hearing. Any committee likes to do something to a bill it is considering. Remember, too," added Pierce, "I'm walking a fine line on this one. Lots of folks in Jefferson County want no change. I can't be too prominent on it. That's why I'm not a sponsor. It's a committee bill, so let's let the committee make any changes and keep me officially out of it."

Part of the fine art of legislation, Pastwell already had discovered, was to let legislators vote one way for the politics back home while maneuvering the other way in the corridors of the Capitol. That was especially true when there was a collision between the preferences back home and the wishes of the gentlemen who provided food, drink and perhaps the outright gift of money, allegedly for future campaigns.

But some legislators still remained an enigma. There didn't seem to be a way to reach them.

Take Senator Jim Hickock, for example. Lots of people thought he must be related to the late Wild Bill Hickok. Maybe he was. The name was not that common. But if he was, Jim Hickock didn't know it. If there was a relationship, it wasn't close like first cousins or nephew/uncle. If it mattered to others, it didn't to the senator.

He represented Jefferson County in the Senate, but Pastwell could not get through to him. He rarely could be found around the Capital Hotel and would not accept the gift of either food or drink when he was.

The only way Pastwell had been able to discuss his point with Hickock was to make an appointment to see him in the Capitol. That unusual arrangement struck Pastwell as an odd way to promote legislation. What did Hickock think the saloon at the Capital Hotel was for?

The senator had been cordial, promised to consider the matter, but beyond that was noncommittal and thereafter not available.

"How do you explain Senator Hickock?" Pastwell asked Pierce.

"A decent fellow. Honest as the day is long. You can't do business with him at all," Pierce had replied.

"But don't worry about it," the representative went on. "He's really obsolete. A throwback to territorial days. His time has passed. He's now in the wrong party. And this is likely his last session. I expect to hold that seat after the next election. You're dealing with an anachronism. Forget him."

Came the day of the hearing and Chairman Pierce asked first for any comments from other members of the House. Representatives Johnson and Eldridge, their participation amply lubricated by Emory Pastwell at the bar of the Capital Hotel, made brief comments in support of the bill. They hoped it could be sped along a bit because of the dire need of the people of the Hunkapapa District for a county of their own.

Chairman Pierce squirmed uneasily in the chair as he watched a group enter the hearing room. It was led by Senator Hickock and consisted of people he recognized from and around Sierra Mesa, but he continued to take testimony in support of the bill.

Emory G. Pastwell was full of praise for the effort.

"This committee is to be congratulated on grasping an urgent problem for the people of the Hunkapapa District of Jefferson County."

There was only one change he would recommend.

"Follow the precedent of Davis County when it was

formed and have the governor appoint a temporary county clerk to take charge of the records until an election can be held. That way the people of the Hunkapapa District don't have to wait for an election for their county to begin serving them."

It gave him smug pleasure to be able to talk about precedents and probe the arcane depths of the law. It made him feel downright professional.

"But what's the hurry?" Representative Aragon wanted to know. "Most counties have been able to wait for an election of officers."

"True, but not all," responded Pastwell. His research in the law was paying off as his confidence swelled. "Most of the laws are different, fashioned I suppose for each circumstance. Hampton County need not wait to get started. There's no point. There's been huge population growth in the area that will be Hampton County. Homesteading saw to that. Gortonville is a long distance from these folks. Every moment of delay is a moment of hardship for them."

When no others spoke for the bill, Chairman Pierce called for the opposition. When none was forthcoming from other representatives he granted the traditional legislative courtesy to members of the other chamber by recognizing Senator Jim Hickock.

"Senator, I gather you are opposed to the bill, 'cause you clearly did not speak for it. And I doubt you're spending your time sitting in this hearing for your health. Would you like now to offer your observations?"

Jim Hickock rose and made his way to the table in front of the committee's desk, where he took the witness chair.

"Thank you, Mr. Chairman, for your courtesy," the senator said. "I ain't sure whether I'm fer or agin' a new county west of the Hunkapapa. But I am bothered by this p'ticular bill and a number of your constituents and mine from around Sierra Mesa are bothered, too. Some of them's the folks come in with me in the back of this here hearin' room today."

"Yes, Senator. Gentlemen from Sierra Mesa, you are most welcome. I always like to work with you. Please proceed, Senator."

"Well, first off," said Hickock, "there's the name. If we gotta have a new county, why call it Hampton? The area this here bill addresses has been known as the Hunkapapa District so long that Hunkapapa would be its obvious name as a county. Then there's the county seat. No other county don't have its seat named by the law. That's up to the folks of the county and their commissioners. And I certainly wouldn't want to rush into nothing, like the last witness proposes. There just ain't no emergency. A new county can wait for an election. Fact is, maybe the question of a county itself ought to go to a vote by all the people in Jefferson County as well as just the people in the Hunkapapa District."

The last suggestion caught all members of the committee off guard. It quickly awakened them from their reveries and refocused their attention on matters at hand.

"But that's unheard of," responded the chairman. "Determining where a county is needed is the responsibility of the legislature and the governor. That's not a matter for an election. No county ever was created by a vote."

"No, Mr. Chairman," replied the senator. "But that don't mean none couldn't be."

Some of the delegation accompanying Senator Hickock offered their testimony when the hearing moved to the general public's turn to cite objections.

"Would you state your name, address and occupation for the record?" the chairman droned as each took the stand. This was new stuff to them, but certainly not to him.

"Ben Baxter. I'm a rancher west of Sierra Mesa."

"Thank you, Mr. Baxter. Please state your position."

"I don't see no need for a new county. But if there is to be one it ought to be called Hunkapapa and I sure don't favor making this new little town, Hampton City, the county seat."

"Why not, Mr. Baxter?" the chairman asked. "If I understand where your ranch is, you'd be a lot closer to Hampton City than Sierra Mesa? Why wouldn't it be in your interest to have a bustling county seat nearby?"

"Well, sir, my loyalties are not necessarily measured in miles.

My town is Sierra Mesa and I intend to keep it that way."

When the next witness stated that he was Henry Guzman, a storekeeper from Sierra Mesa, the chairman asked:

"Do you think you might possibly have a conflict of interest as the founder of Sierra Mesa, which it is my understanding you are, and the first mayor, which it is my understanding you were?"

"I didn't found Sierra Mesa. I opened a country store that I called the Sierra Mesa because I liked the sound of the name and the town grew up around it. Sure, I was the first mayor, right after we incorporated back in the days of territory, but just because folks asked me to be. I don't see how that gave me a conflict."

"Nonetheless, you have a financial interest in seeing Sierra Mesa succeed and Hampton City fail, am I right, Mr. Guzman?"

"You are not right, Mr. Representative. As a storekeeper, I have a financial interest wherever I am. I could pack up and move to Hampton City if I wanted. I choose not to. My loyalties lie with Sierra Mesa. Like Ben Baxter doesn't measure his in miles, I don't measure mine in dollars."

The opposition from the Sierra Mesa community was pointed, adamant and unanimous. No county. But if there is to be a county, vote on it. Name it Hunkapapa and let the people choose the county seat.

Representative Aragon, who was starting to get under the chairman's skin, observed that the testimony from people living in the Hunkapapa District hardly coincided with earlier claims of a dire emergency and severe hardship.

"If the people who live there aren't aware of their hardship, Mr. Chairman, I see no reason for this committee to be panicked into saving them from it."

What particularly irked S. Franklin Pierce was that Aragon was right. The chairman was all too well aware that most counties were formed only after the people who lived there showed by petition or personal appeal that most of them desperately wanted a county of their own. He couldn't understand why Emory Pastwell had not been ready with a strong show of support from Hampton City.

But before this line of reasoning could take root, Chairman Pierce closed the hearing by thanking the good people of Sierra Mesa for going to the expense and trouble of coming to the Capitol and offering their opinions on the bill before them.

"I assure you this committee will give very serious consideration to the concerns you have raised, very serious," he said.

Pastwell was visibly shaken. The case against his bill had been strong, stronger perhaps than the case for it. He sought out Representative Pierce as soon as he prudently could.

"Don't worry about it." The chairman was reassuring. "We've just gone through the motions. I may have to vote no on the floor, but this bill is greased. It will sail through the House with your amendment for a temporary county clerk."

And it did. Representatives honored legislative custom with the pretense of a brief debate. Representative Pierce said nothing, voted no when his time came, but he had done his work well and the final vote was a convincing 53-19 with three excused.

Representative Pierce had one final warning for his friend. When the bill comes up for a hearing in the Senate, be sure to offset opposition from Sierra Mesa with a vigorous demonstration by an array of backers in Hampton City.

"You should have had them on hand for the hearing in my committee," he lectured.

"I wish you had reminded me."

"Well, it's really not my duty. It's yours. 'Course if I'd known a delegation was coming over from Sierra Mesa, I might have mentioned it."

"I didn't know they were coming either," Pastwell said, thinking again there was no way to work with Senator Hickock.

"Well, it's over with on this side," Chairman Pierce said. "But remember to try to give the Senate the impression that it's just a vocal minority who are causing trouble. They're just being childish because their town is losing out. Most people in the affected territory want a county urgently. That's the point you have to pound home in the Senate."

Emory Pastwell allowed himself a brief celebration after the House vote. But only a brief one, for the work was only half done. Now came the Senate. Pastwell had no well-placed ally, like Representative S. Franklin Pierce, in the Senate.

Try as he might, he could not seem to develop such a crony. Senator Jim Hickock was absolutely no help. His ranch was on the west bank of the Hunkapapa River. Thus, he lived in what would become the new county, represented the area, and was not friendly to the cause.

The trouble was, the other senators kept deferring to him. He was in the minority party and wasn't even on the appropriate committee. To Pastwell, his crude speech and rough features made him out the yokel. Pastwell would have been tempted to dismiss him as a meaningless rube if it weren't for a power he appeared to possess that Pastwell could not fathom. Whatever the source of his power, he did not seem to be the anachronism Pierce had made him out to be. Ignoring him, as Pierce suggested, no longer seemed prudent at all.

Had he been more of a veteran viewer of the legislature, Pastwell would have known that the Senate was like a club. Members looked after their own. That explained part of Hickock's stature. But it didn't explain the rest. Jim Hickock was just plain respected both for his personal integrity and his standing as one of the men who truly made a difference in acquiring statehood.

His persuasive appeal to a meeting of Western congressmen on the reason that it was time for the territory to become a state had become legendary around the Capitol. It was widely held that his speech was even more eloquent than it was ungrammatical.

The hearing on the Hampton County bill told the difference Pastwell faced between the House and the Senate. In the ornate hearing room where Senator Charles Garrison presided behind a high desk with a very formal-looking gavel in hand, Senator Jim Hickock and his constituents from Sierra Mesa were treated like the guests of honor.

Procedure called for proponents to be heard first, but this bill affected Hickock's home territory. Therefore, the senator and his constituents would be granted the senatorial privilege of leading off in the hearing.

Hickock went through his concerns point by point. He wasn't sure that there should be another county, but if there should, it ought to be established by a vote of the people. It shouldn't be named Hampton but rather Hunkapapa, and the county seat should not be part of the law.

"But that would just continue another Indian name," observed Senator William Hochsler. "Don't we have enough of them already?"

"Well, Bill," replied Jim Hickock, "reckon the Indians was here before we were and got to name things first. Fact is, though, the Sioux never called the river or the district Hunkapapa. We white folks did that, and we did so I think out of respect for a proud and great people."

"How you call them savages proud and great?" demanded Hochsler.

"Now, Bill, I know there was a lot of friction between the whites and the Indians that's still mighty fresh in some of our minds. But I'm tellin' you that the Hunkapapa Sioux are a great people and we whites will come to recognize that in time. They sure come up with some kind of leader in Sittin' Bull that some of us come to respect the hard way. Well, now, before his days come to an untimely end, Sittin' Bull hisself put that conflict behind him enough to go tour with Bill Cody and that daffy Wild West show of his. I think we whites can put it behind us, too. Someday our children or grandchildren will be glad we did. We oughta simply stick to the old, familiar name, Hunkapapa."

Others from Sierra Mesa echoed Senator Hickock's testimony. This time it was Ted Fullmer's turn to speak for the ranchers. He and Ben Baxter couldn't get away at the same time. One had to stay behind to tend to chores at both ranches when the other went somewhere. His testimony was the same.

Pastwell was visibly subdued. He didn't even object when the opposition was heard first in a reversal of legislative order. Since the senators had done that for a fellow senator, he was not about to make a point of it. He no longer spoke of hardships and urgent problems for people in western Jefferson County, which could be relieved only by formation of a new county.

He simply made a reserved pitch for keeping his pet bill in the form passed by the House.

"The bill before you serves a noble purpose for all of the people in what would be the new county. I am sure that even those who object to it today would soon relate to the benefits of having a county of their own. I respectfully request that you report this bill out with a do-pass recommendation in the form in which you received it from the House."

He was politely received, but dismissed following his testimony without a question.

He had managed to persuade two persons from Hampton City to be on hand to speak for the bill. Hamilton Jones, the first storekeeper to gamble on the new town, and George Heartily, a leader of the homesteaders nearby, both testified. They were, however, somewhat intimidated by the vigorous opposition from their senator and Sierra Mesa neighbors. Nor were they buoyed by Emory Pastwell, who was so thoroughly deflated he lacked his usual peddler's show of confidence. They spoke of the convenience of a county of their own and ducked out thankful that they didn't have to field questions.

"Jim," said the chairman to Hickock, having gone through the required procedure of allowing the other side to state its case, "my reading of this committee is that we will send a bill to the floor to let the full Senate decide on whether the western portion of Jefferson County ought to be another county.

"You and I have had and continue to have our political differences. Guess that's why we belong to different parties. But you and I have also stood side by side enough for me to know I'd rather work with you than against you. If it wasn't for you, we might still be a territorial legislature. So I'm gonna tell you, I think the committee will send this bill to the floor with a county named Hunkapapa, a vote of the people to establish it, and no county seat named."

"Thank you, Charlie," said Jim Hickock.

"But, Mr. Chairman," objected Emory Pastwell.

"Hearing adjourned," said the chairman with a hard rap of the gavel.

The bill from the House was amended in committee just as the chairman had indicated and sent to a vote on the Senate floor. Senator Hickock told his colleagues that he still wasn't sure Jefferson County ought to be divided or that the new county west of the Hunkapapa River would endure over time as a workable unit of government.

"I couldn't support no bill that just dictated a county where there ain't one now if the people ain't interested," he said.

"Terrible grammar for a senator," whispered the young reporter to the old reporter.

"Son," replied the old reporter, "I've been covering the legislature long enough to know the right use of the King's English doesn't necessarily have anything to do with intelligence. Jim Hickock may not be well-educated, but he's one of the savviest men and most honorable, too, who ever stood on that floor. You shoulda heard him speak to a bunch of congressmen one time when…"

"I know, I know," the young reporter interrupted. "The statehood speech. I'm getting sick of hearing about it."

"But I can support this bill on this floor today," Hickock assured his colleagues. "If a new county is to be formed, it will have to be approved by all of the voters of Jefferson County and also have a separate majority in the Hunkapapa District that would become the new county. If the voters are for it, I'm sure enough willin' to give it a try."

Senator Hickock was in the minority party, but he nonetheless was one of the most widely respected members of the Senate. Even those who thought he went overboard on integrity admired him for it.

The vote was unanimous forty-three to nothing with two excused.

"It's a disaster," declared a distraught Emory G. Pastwell. "That bill now is worse than no bill."

"Easy, my friend," soothed Representative S. Franklin Pierce. "Still takes two houses to pass legislation."

"But what do we do? How can we get our bill back?"

"I assure you I'll be on the conference committee. Now, we may not get everything. But we'll get a good enough compromise to serve your purposes."

A conference committee, another dark hole in the treacherous and baffling path of legislation. Emory Pastwell had to learn that, no, he would not be given a chance to address the conference. The committee's sole purpose was to iron out differences between the two chambers. He could, of course, continue to work the bar at the Capital Hotel.

The conference committee strived mightily to resolve the differences between the House and the Senate and for a time seemed deadlocked.

"What is it that's most important to you?" the Senate side finally asked in exasperation of its House counterparts.

"That we establish a new county here and now and do it as responsible legislators, not pass the buck to the voters," replied Pierce. "What's yours?"

"That we stick to the name Hunkapapa instead of Hampton and that we leave it to the people of the new county to designate their county seat," responded Senator Garrison after a quick consultation with Jim Hickock.

And so the issue was resolved and both houses approved a bill that established Hunkapapa County effective July 1, with a temporary county clerk to be appointed by the governor, election of officers to be held two months later, and the county seat not to be named in the law.

"That's not what we set out for," complained a baffled and frustrated Pastwell. "Where's Hampton County? Where's the county seat?"

Representative Pierce consoled and reassured him. "Now take it easy, Emory. You got most of what you wanted. You have a county. Maybe it doesn't have the name you would have preferred. But it is a county."

"But there's no county seat?"

"Why do you worry? This is the boost you wanted for Hampton City. Who else is going to challenge for the seat? Sierra Mesa? They're not even organized. You're way ahead of them. Besides, the governor owes me one. I'll ask him to designate Hampton City as the temporary seat when he declares it to be an organized county and appoints the temporary clerk. If I were you, I'd build a courthouse fast in your town square and seal the future of Hampton City right there."

So there it was. There would be a new county. Emory Pastwell had to find a way to tell his brother-in-law, Otis P. Hampton, that it wouldn't bear the family name. But at least there would be no vote, the county would be instantly created and he should be able to throw up a structure that could serve as a courthouse by the time the county records arrived on the first of July.

He'd just have to live with Hunkapapa County as his brainchild's name and use his wits instead of the law to make Hampton City the county seat that would give it the thrust it needed to achieve its potential. He had his sales gimmick practically in hand.

SIX

The initial reaction to the new county in the Sierra Mesa community was positively negative. Adamantly negative. That included the whole community, not just the town of Sierra Mesa, but also all of the country folk around. It wasn't the idea of a new county that got them, but what it would do to their town.

They knew that Emory G. Pastwell was out to do in Sierra Mesa. His purpose was clear: to drive Sierra Mesa's businesses into Hampton City and force its population to follow. It was bad enough to lose the place they called the home town. But to have it happen by the guile of a city slicker from the East added insult to injury.

What really hurt was to imagine him snickering to himself over snookering a bunch of hicks. What hurt even more was to admit that he probably was doing exactly that, that they were the hicks on the losing end of the slicker's slick chicanery.

Only the small pocket in Hampton City and a handful of homesteaders on its outskirts stood in favor of the scheme. They assumed they had nothing to lose and a lot to gain by forming a county with Hampton City as the county seat.

But as time passed and folks pondered the situation, Sierra Mesa's opposition began to soften, slightly at first, even subtly. From the time the legislature adjourned around the end of February until the county would be official July 1, there was plenty of time for people to rethink their original reaction.

Local folks were still concerned about being had, or appearing to be had. An eastern dandy had put a county over on them despite their best objections to their own legislature and he just might succeed in destroying Sierra Mesa in the process.

But gradually it occurred to them that Emory Pastwell had not been as slick as he thought he was. The fact is, old Jim Hickock outwitted him. And Senator Hickock's friends and neighbors were more than relieved that they didn't have the Hampton name imposed on them against their will, or the designation of Hampton City as county seat shoved down their throats. That would have been hard to swallow.

Oh, they supposed Hampton City would become county seat anyway, but at least it wasn't forced by law. So they were pleased, as they thought about it, maybe even smug, because one of their own had turned the tables—at least a couple of the tables—on the dude from the East.

They still worried about Sierra Mesa, for they were well aware that Pastwell's designs on their town remained unchanged. He still intended that Hampton City would take over its people and its commerce. Hampton City! Just another nondescript name chosen for some obscure railroad executive. What was to become of the musical Spanish name for their town that they enjoyed so much?

But that was another matter. On the issue at hand, a new county was beginning to make a great deal of sense to a lot of the people in and around Sierra Mesa.

For one thing, Gortonville was a long ways away. If you

had county business, and everybody did at one time or another, you had to block out at least a day just to go to the courthouse to tend to it. And that's if you caught the eastbound train in the morning and got business taken care of in time to catch the westbound train in the afternoon.

Before the railroad came through, you had to take at least two days to tend to county affairs, which was still true for those who eschewed rails in favor of horse.

For another thing, the Hunkapapa District had very little in common with the rest of Jefferson County. Funny thing about the Hunkapapa River. It sliced up more than the land. It also separated the culture, even the agriculture.

East of the river, the farming brought in by the homesteaders now was more prevalent than the ranching that had dominated previously. The life style was more like that of the newcomers than the original settlers.

They had come from Iowa, Illinois, Indiana, in other words mainly from the Midwest. They brought with them the rigid religious ways of the Bible Belt they had just left. They also transplanted Midwestern-style grain farming and Republican politics. They did not populate the saloons on Saturday night, not overtly anyway, or fail to fill the church pews on Sunday morning, at least not often. They were in stark contrast to the irreverent spirits of the earlier Western settlers.

West of the river, ranching dominated agriculture and the economy. It also defined the prevalent way of life. Most of the homesteaders either sold out to established ranchers or started buying up neighboring homesteads to incorporate them into ranches of their own. The newcomers who stayed tended to adopt the way of life of the old timers. Most of them could even be found in saloons on Saturday night and their strict religious habits began to loosen a bit.

They even got so they understood and appreciated the wisdom of free coinage of silver as advocated by the ranking political hero, William Jennings Bryant, who had been the Democratic Party's nominee in the last presidential election. Gold alone was not able to fill the needs of the economy. The overvalued dollar multiplied debts. "Free Silver" was a rallying cry they could answer. Therefore, many of the newcomers identified with the established ranchers, who tended to be Democrats. But mostly they were an independent lot who relished the current wave of Populism that Bryant personified, for he also had been the nominee of the People's Party.

And then there was the matter of influence. The rest of Jefferson County more or less ignored the Hunkapapa District. County officials came from east of the river. Their interests lay in eastern Jefferson County. Western Jefferson County was good for taxes and maybe a few votes and little else.

The people of the Hunkapapa District had to fend for themselves. They received virtually no county services. Only in the case of a crime that had to be investigated did the Hunkapapa people ever see a deputy sheriff. The sheriff himself might make a swing through just before an election, but that would be the end of his footprints in the Hunkapapa District until the next election.

So maybe a county of their own wasn't such a bad idea, the folks began to believe, especially if it wouldn't cost more in taxes than they were already sending to Gortonville.

They even started to resign themselves to having the courthouse in Hampton City. They didn't like it. But, sore point that it was, there didn't seem to be much they could do about it.

As the days drew down toward the first of July when on that summer Saturday Hunkapapa County would become a reality, people were starting to get a little excited about it. There was an air of mystery around the governmental metamorphosis that was transpiring. They didn't really understand what a county would look like.

It would still be the same land. The river would become a county line, but the stream wouldn't change. No one would paint a stripe down the middle of the channel. Odd, it was, how those boundaries that designated counties, or towns for that matter, could carry so much weight in the affairs of men, yet be so hard to see. You'd think there would be a line across the land, like there is on a map, but in fact boundaries were invisible.

Word went out that a Great Lakes Pacific train would be bringing the records from Gortonville a few days before Hunkapapa County became a fact. The westbound train would pass through Sierra Mesa on a Friday afternoon on the way to Hampton City, where the records would sit in a car on a side track until they could be moved into the wooden structure being thrown together by Emory G. Pastwell to serve as a courthouse.

At long last, people would have a chance to see for themselves what a county was. They'd be coming from miles around to be at the depot in Sierra Mesa when the train stopped to take on water before passing through.

Out our way, Dad had decreed a holiday. We were all going to town on Friday. Friday! Imagine! Saturday was when we went to town. But despite his misgivings about a county that made Hampton City the county seat, he suspected that history was in the making.

"We'll never have another chance like it," he thundered. "It'll be an education for the kids. They'll see a county in the making, formed before their very own eyes."

Mom was less enthusiastic, a bit skeptical even of the significance of the occasion. "Well, maybe," she said. "But we've been around when lots of counties have been created. They make new ones every two years."

"We never lived where they was amakin' one before," responded her husband.

My sister and I were both pulling for Dad. It would be something to see that train. But just imagine going to town on Friday.

To tell the truth, it wasn't really an argument between Mom and Dad. Mom wasn't insistent or anything like that. I suspect she also liked the idea of going to town on Friday. And she was probably curious, too, about what a county looked like. She was simply trying to keep the occasion in perspective.

She just wasn't as convinced as Dad that the event ranked somewhere with Moses coming down from the mountain top, Washington crossing the Delaware or even Jim Hickock's eloquent, if ungrammatical, appeal to Western congressmen that it was time for the territory to become a state.

But she had become as excited as the rest of us when the day arrived, Friday, the 23rd day of June just one year before a new century took over from the old one and a full week before the Hunkapapa District turned into Hunkapapa County. All members of the Baxter family put on our going-to-town clothes. Mom, Dad, Sis and I climbed aboard the wagon to which Dad had hitched a team of horses and we headed the nine miles east and one mile north to Sierra Mesa.

No sooner were we on the trail than we spotted a little dust cloud over toward the Fullmer ranch to the north. We soon caught up with the Fullmers, who were doing the same thing. We stopped long enough for me to shift over to the Fullmers' wagon to ride with Becky while her kid brother switched over to our wagon to join my little sister.

The Fullmers and Baxters were so close we were more like family than neighbors. Dad and Ted Fullmer had been boyhood friends and they cowboyed together when they were young. I think maybe they did a few other things together they wouldn't tolerate in their own children. I got the impression from things I picked up that I wasn't supposed to hear that they were pretty wild young buckaroos. That changed when the two young ladies who were also girlhood friends got them under their spell, married them, and settled them down on their home ranches.

We traveled across the high plateau side by side in great good humor. Wisecracks were flying back and forth between fathers.

"See you ain't been able to give that roan away yet."

"Nope. But I suppose you want to trade that whole team for her."

Gentler comments passed between mothers.

"That's a beautiful outfit, Nellie. Where'd you get it?"

"Why, thank you, Sally. I made it the best I could remember after that gorgeous dress you were wearing at the school social," Mom replied. "You know the one I mean?"

"Oh, I know the one," laughed Mrs. Fullmer. "My wardrobe's not so big that I don't know all three dresses in it."

"Why, you're the best-dressed woman in the Hunkapapa District," Mom said. "If you only have three dresses you surely get the most out of them."

"I'd be proud to be as well-dressed as you, Nellie."

Mr. Fullmer winked at Dad: "She only has three dresses, all right. Three for each day of the week."

"I know," Dad nodded. "I've looked in my wife's closet, too."

Mrs. Fullmer feigned indignation. "What hope is there?" she said to Mom. "Think they'll ever amount to anything?"

"Heaven knows, we've tried, Sally," Mom replied. "I think the good Lord will give us credit for that."

Time passed so quickly that we reached the road in what seemed a record. For the last mile when we were off the trail and onto the road going into town we had to go single file so as to leave room if anybody was going the other way. The Fullmers swung in front and we dropped in behind them.

Our two families sure weren't alone. Everybody from the western end of the Hunkapapa District seemed to be going to town on Friday instead of Saturday this week. Chances are that was equally true from all other directions out of Sierra Mesa, too. The town was so crowded with people and horses and wagons it must have been true that no one stayed home. Why, it was busier than it usually was on Saturdays.

We gathered with everyone else at the depot to wait for the westbound Great Lakes Pacific train.

Men kept checking their watches. "Shudda been here ten minutes ago," Dad muttered.

Mr. Fullmer dutifully took out his watch and read it. "Yep. By my watch maybe even twelve minutes ago."

The place was jumping with nervousness, excitement, anticipation, mystery and a degree of apprehension.

One man got down on his hands and knees and put his ear to the rail. "She's on her way," he declared knowingly. "I can hear her."

The first sharp ear to pick up the chug-chug of the steam engine belonged to Henry Guzman, the storekeeper who gave Sierra Mesa its name.

"Here she comes!" he shouted.

Normally a storekeeper wouldn't take time away from his shop when the country people came to town. But today none of the customers was buying yet. That would come later. Knowing as much, the merchants all shut down for a while so they and their help could join in the excitement.

Sure enough, the big engine pulling only a few cars chugged into view. The engineer gave the whistle a heavier workout than usual, greeting the gathering throng and acknowledging his own prominent role in this historic event.

The train lumbered to a stop with the locomotive hard by the water tower where it could take on more water to finish the trip to Hampton City.

The engineer, now filled with self-importance, was motioning with all the vigor his arm could stand to indicate which car we were interested in.

"Fourth one down," he hollered, trying to make his prominent self heard over the roar of his engine.

The door opened to the fourth box car while the crowd pressed in. There to greet them was a well-known face as State Representative S. Franklin Pierce seized the opportunity to display his superior presence before a sizable gathering of his constituents.

"Welcome to Hunkapapa County," he bellowed, as he bowed low, sweeping his top hat near the floor of the car and then pointing it toward the object of interest to the assembled masses.

Box after box of books and papers took up only a corner of a nearly empty box car. There was a deputy sheriff riding as an armed guard to protect the records that would be transmitted from Jefferson County to the new Hunkapapa County. Mostly they consisted of property papers, deeds, titles, mortgages, liens, that sort of thing, and taxes, of course, both those paid and those in arrears. There were a few documents of marriages, births, deaths and divorces collected by the county to pass on to the state. And there were some court records. That was it. A lot of paper, but nothing substantial or dramatic to herald the official formation of a new county.

Everybody looked somewhat amazed and a little disappointed. We were here for a historic moment. There never had been a county here before and now there would be one for all time. And all we could see was a bunch of boxes.

"Is that all a county amounts to?" asked someone up close to the boxcar's door.

The crowd began to disperse. Everyone had a chance to walk past the open door and take a look up close. Facial expressions clearly indicated that everybody felt let down after all the buildup.

"Some county," groaned Ted Fullmer to his pal, my Dad, Ben Baxter. "You could put the whole thing in a wagon."

He no sooner said it than he looked at my father and my father looked at him and an expression of instant enlightenment swept over their eyes.

"You could put the whole thing in a wagon," my Dad said with pointed emphasis, repeating his friend and neighbor for effect as the significance of the observation began to sink in.

"Henry," he shouted after Mr. Guzman. The storekeeper turned around, a bit anxiously for he knew now that the country folks were about to do their shopping and he had better get to the store.

"Henry, Hampton City don't need to be our county seat. We can collect them county records neat as not and make Sierra Mesa county seat of Hunkapapa County."

The enormity of the scheme began to catch Henry Guzman's imagination. "You mean," he stopped as he contemplated it. "You mean steal 'em?"

"I mean take our county records and keep 'em in Sierra Mesa," Dad replied. "We got as much right to 'em as Hampton City. Likely more. We been here longer. We wouldn't be breakin' no law, just takin' what's rightfully ours."

"Well, now, I dunno. Maybe." Henry Guzman was interested, but worried. He also was fretting about trade he might be missing. "But I gotta get back to the store."

"No, listen," Mr. Fullmer interrupted. "There'll be lots of days to shop, but not many to take our county back. You get the word out to a few town folks you can trust to do a job and keep it to theirselves and we'll sort out a few of the ranchers. We'll gather at Ed Duggin's place in half an hour."

Ed Duggin ran the Hunkapapa Saloon, the largest of the four in town. It was a favorite gathering place for the men of the town and also for the country men when they went to town.

Of course, it was less than a favorite of the women. One reason was that what went on there on Saturdays made their husbands unpleasant to put up with for a time and hard to get to church on Sundays.

But the history of the place also disturbed them. They knew that Ed Duggin started it as kind of a general pleasure palace. In addition to the saloon he had a few rooms upstairs that could be rented for a night's sleep. Or, more commonly, they could be rented for a little more cash with the companionship of the gentler sex.

The fact is, Ed's original sign said Hunkapapa Saloon and Whorehouse. Even in the earliest of times, the sign drew some criticism. Folks pointed out that whorehouses in other towns didn't actually use the term. They were called "Edna's Rooms," after the madams who ran them, or "Rooms for Gentlemen." They didn't come right out and say what they were. But Ed rejected such euphemism as hypocritical. He figured he might just as well be honest about it and advertise his wares openly on his sign.

In recent years, though, there had been such a protest that he not only had no ladies of the night on hand, but he also had let the word "whorehouse" fade from his sign until it was barely visible.

The community's attitude was more of a puzzle to him than a business setback.

"Some of the most outspoken women of the community came to this town for jobs in my establishment and got their start working in those rooms," he'd explain.

"Yeah," a customer would say, maybe even one who had married one of Ed's girls. "They came because they didn't see anything else to do. But they've settled in. They helped bring civilization to Sierra Mesa and want it to be a respectable community for their children."

It was true that many of the leading ladies of the town came to the area to provide the sexual pleasures that Ed Duggin offered for a fee. No one talked much about it, or even speculated on whose wives and mothers—or grandmothers—had been among Ed's lovely employees.

Times had changed, they had changed with them, maybe even pushing the change a bit. Their past, if shady, was past. They were now ladies, homemakers, and determined parents, or grandparents.

Ed had tried for a while to use the rooms strictly as a hotel, no feminine companionship offered. But what demand there may have been for the hotel rooms he could supply vanished completely when the Great Lakes Pacific Railroad opened its new and modern hotel down by the station.

So Ed Duggin's place was strictly a saloon now, a meeting place for the men of the community. And the men gathered, maybe a dozen, hand-picked. They would be the ones who had the gumption and the ability to undertake a mission for their community, and keep their mouths shut about it until it was over.

This much they knew. The car carrying the county records would be parked on a side track after it got to Hampton City today. It would sit there until the papers could be moved into the wood structure Emory Pastwell was throwing up. He was determined to have it far enough along to move the boxes into it by the following Saturday when Hunkapapa became a county and the governor sent a temporary clerk there to take charge.

That meant they had only a week to act.

"In fact," my Dad had said, "We really only have a day."

The others looked at him in amazement. Why only a day?

"Tomorrow's Saturday," he said as if that ought to be explanation enough.

"So?" His reasoning wasn't immediately clear to Henry Guzman.

"Saturday's the time to strike. We all know what the men around here do on Saturday night. Well, we won't do it. We'll all take a vow to stay sober. Sorry about that, Ed. The men in Hampton City who are guarding the county will do their usual Saturday night boozin'.

"We go over there cold sober, with a team and wagon and enough men to move the records in a minute or two, but not so many that we stumble over each other. Then we bust out of there while they're all snookered up. It's our best chance to pull it off."

So it was agreed. A half a dozen men would gather at our place. Dad and Ted Fullmer would take a wagon guarded by four men on horseback into Hampton City, grab the county and head as fast as they could push the horses to Sierra Mesa.

Another half dozen men would stand by at the road entering Sierra Mesa to provide a well-armed welcoming committee if the Hampton City crowd were in hot pursuit.

The deputy sheriff riding shotgun for the county records provided some concern. No one wanted to get in trouble with the law. But he surely wouldn't be with the boxes all the time. Maybe it was just his job to get the documents to their destination, not to baby-sit them afterward. Maybe he would at least take a Saturday night break to join the rest of the men in Hampton City at the bar.

But in any event, it was none of his business. He was Jefferson County and this was Hunkapapa County business.

Ed Duggin bought a round on the house so the men could all toast the notion of a sober Saturday night. They sealed their deal with a handshake all around. Then they went their separate ways toward a joint goal of outsmarting an Eastern dandy one more time and saving Sierra Mesa while they were at it.

SEVEN

The Fullmers arrived early Saturday afternoon. Our place was the staging area for the campaign to claim Sierra Mesa's rightful role in Hunkapapa County.

We had even better access than the Fullmers to Hampton City about three miles away. We could get most of the way to the new town without anyone seeing us coming. Only the last mile, where the land rises by the old hole in the ground that used to be the cellar of a store, does Hampton City come into view.

I could tell Mrs. Fullmer was as apprehensive as Mom had been about the venture. Both of them thought that long ago they had house-broken the wild, young buckaroos they had married.

Dad hadn't asked Mom. He just told her.

"A bunch of us got together in town and decided Sierra Mesa is the rightful county seat of our new county and we're going to do something about it. Ted and me and some of the others are going to gather here and take a wagon into Hampton City to get the records, so get ready for company."

The latter didn't concern her. Company was always welcome. But the first part did. It was the kind of stunt he might have pulled in his younger days. She thought her husband was now a settled-down family man and the notion of him getting involved in a raid that invited gunfire sent shudders up and down her spine.

"Isn't that kind of crazy?" she'd protested. "I mean, that's picking a fight and stealing something that doesn't belong to us."

"'Course it belongs to us," he had responded sharply. "Belongs to Hunkapapa County and that's us. Someone has to look after our interests. Can't just let a pretty boy from Chicago bully us around and kill off our community the way he's trying to."

"But, Benjamin." She only called him Benjamin when she was exasperated with him, as some Saturday nights. Otherwise, he was just Ben or more likely Dear or Hon or Lover. "There's likely to be fighting, shooting. You could get killed, and for what? It's not worth it. What would become of me and the children?"

But he wasn't having any of it. "We're going to go take back our county and keep it in Sierra Mesa and that's that. I'm goin' to do it for you and the children as much as anything. Our home is part of this here community. So savin' the community is also savin' our home."

And that was that. I got the impression that the Fullmers had had a similar discussion, especially when Mom and Mrs. Fullmer holed up in the kitchen by themselves and you could hear the tone of anxiety in a private conversation so quiet it was almost carried on in whispers.

We'd pick up only snatches. "Crazy galoots." "Scared to death." Snippets like that.

Their husbands were having just as serious a conversation as they looked over the draft horses currently in from the range and available for duty. They were trying to decide whether to hitch up a four-horse team or a two-horse team.

"With all those boxes of papers, we'll have a heavy enough load," Dad acknowledged.

"But nothing a couple of horses can't handle," Mr. Fullmer said. "'Course, if we get caught in a chase, two horses wouldn't last very long."

"True," Dad agreed. "On the other hand, four plug horses might last longer, but they still couldn't outrun men on saddle horses."

"That's right," his neighbor responded. "And four horses would attract attention. Folks have to have a reason to hitch up four horses just to go to town."

"I reckon the four riders will attract attention, too," Dad said, pondered the thought for a moment, then added, "but they can disperse a little bit so they're not quite so conspicuous. Couldn't do that with a four-horse team."

In the end Dad and Mr. Fullmer settled on a pair of big, strong geldings, then checked and rechecked the team and wagon they had selected for the venture. They didn't want something like a busted wheel or lame horse or a worn harness strap to spoil the plan.

"Never can predict these things," Dad had said. "Something can go wrong with a wagon or a horse at any time. But this looks about as certain as anything can be."

"Looks solid to me, Ben," Ted Fullmer replied.

Nonetheless, they kept going over and over the wagon and the harness.

The four horsemen who were selected to ride with them arrived by late afternoon. One had a piece of good news.

"The eastbound train went through this morning. Folks at the depot saw the deputy wave to them as it went through."

So there would be no deputy sheriff to worry about. He rode shotgun on the records from Gortonville to Hampton City. His job was done. So now it was between the settled community of Sierra Mesa and Emory G. Pastwell's upstart town.

One of the riders, another neighbor, rode through Hampton City before coming over. He said the box car was on the side track just where it was supposed to be. When he went by, the door was ajar. That meant at that time at least it was unlocked. Another part of the plan was falling satisfactorily into place.

Mom and Mrs. Fullmer served everybody a big supper of beef in gravy and boiled potatoes with baking soda biscuits and topped off with apple pie.

Becky and I thought we'd go for a ride to work off the meal, which seemed fine with parents all around. They didn't worry about us riding around the range. It was just a big playground and we were comfortably familiar with maybe a hundred square miles of it.

Furthermore, I think they were just as glad to have us out of the way. Our mothers because they really didn't want us to know what was going on, and our fathers because they didn't want us to be involved.

But we knew full well what the plans were. They would ride out about sunset so they could get to the side track in Hampton City under the cover of the gathering darkness. There would be just enough dusk left to give them a dim view of their quarry in the boxcar so they could see what they were doing. They would load the boxes fast and move out for Sierra Mesa. The gentle light from the moon and stars would be enough to guide them, especially over terrain that Ben Baxter and Ted Fullmer knew like the backs of their hands.

If all went well, that would be all there was to it. They would naturally be prepared to pry open a boxcar door, should that be necessary, and to club a watchman over the head, gently of course, if one were posted.

But they figured the element of surprise, the cover of darkness and the Saturday night drinking habits would enable them to complete their task unnoticed. Sometime through the hangover of a Sunday morning, Hampton City would discover that it no longer possessed the county records.

Becky and I headed straight for our hangout. We'd have plenty of daylight for a little play. We tied up the horses deep on a horseweed trail by the old corral, then unstrapped our lariats before heading for the hole in the ground.

We had taken lately to a friendly competition with our

ropes and we were just beginning to get good at it. We weren't doing too well hitting targets while on the move at a full gallop, but using a rope from a horse would come later. First we had to learn how to handle the lasso standing still. We were hitting targets with increasing regularity as we picked them out around our horseweed forest, the old corral and the basement of the erstwhile country store.

We probably would have headed to our favorite spot regardless, but there was further method to our madness. If we fudged the time to get home just a little, our hole in the ground would give us the closest thing to a front-row seat for the rescue operation our fathers were engaged in.

"Here they come," Becky announced in a shouted whisper when she first caught a glimpse of movement through the dusk.

We ducked down in our hole in the ground where our fathers or their companions couldn't see us and we stayed low and out of sight as they rode by so close to our hideout we could almost reach out and touch them. In fact they were so close we could have roped them.

The moment of truth was at hand. They were on their way to Hampton City.

As it turned out, their plan looked flawless. They rode into Hampton City as dusk was turning to night. The saloon was aroar with activity as the men in and around the new town took to their normal Saturday night pastime.

But no one was around the depot. The box car sat on a side track just as expected. The door was closed, but not even locked.

"No watchman," Ted Fullmer said quietly but pointedly. No one was standing guard. That was a big help.

Dad drove the wagon right up to the door, and the six of them hurriedly went about shifting boxes from box car to wagon box. The four horsemen were carrying boxes from the box car. Dad and Mr. Fullmer were stacking them safely in the wagon. In only minutes, they were starting to pull away from the railroad and it looked like clear sailing all the way to Sierra Mesa.

At that moment, two dandies appeared from the door of the

hotel. They were obviously far enough into a Saturday night bottle to be slightly unsteady. But they weren't reeling too badly as they started for the saloon to complete the Saturday night spree. Caught in the importance of their conversation, they weren't paying much attention to the traffic. They stepped into the street so abruptly that Dad had to rein in the team hard to keep from hitting them.

"Beg your pardon," slurred Emory G. Pastwell.

"Evening, folks. Sorry to 'sturb you," said state Representative S. Franklin Pierce.

"No problem," Dad had said. But the moment they were past, he snapped the reins and the horses took off fast.

Suddenly Emory Pastwell pulled up with a start. The probability of what just happened was beginning to penetrate a mildly besotted brain.

"Hold it," he yelled. "Stop! Come back here!"

Of course Dad and his entourage kept on going. Faster.

"What is it?" asked Pierce. Perhaps only because the matter did not have the same import that it had for Pastwell, he hadn't caught on yet.

Pastwell ran for the siding, shouting, "I think we've been robbed!"

He reached the parked box car. The door stood open. He peered in through the darkness, but couldn't make out shapes. Finally he struck a match. The glow provided enough light to confirm his worst fears. The box car was empty.

"The county's been robbed," he yelled.

He ran for the saloon, shouting at the top of his voice, "The county's been robbed! The county's been robbed! After the robbers, men! After them!"

Over the din of the saloon, the men of Hampton City heard the shout. Then, as if in unison after a long minute for the message to wade through the haze of too many drinks, they understood its urgency.

They burst out the door as best a bunch of drunks could do, several trying to penetrate the opening at the same time. Those who had horses stumbled over one another as they untied their mounts and flung themselves unsteadily onto their saddles. Others took off hopelessly afoot.

"After them, men!" Pastwell was barking orders. "They went that way! After them!"

Back in our hole in the ground, Becky and I peacefully sat through all of the dramatics, little imagining the peril our fathers now were facing. We were a little tense, of course, because the plan was a bit daring, but we fully expected it to go off without a hitch.

Suddenly we were shaken to our senses when we picked up a disturbing sound. There was something frantic about it. As our eyes focused through the starlight on distant objects, we made out the shape of a wagon and a cluster of horses moving fast. They were heading toward us at top speed. The team was being urged to do more than it should, or could. Even good horses like those could not keep up the pace all the way to Sierra Mesa. That would be asking too much of good saddle horses, let alone the work horses that were pulling a wagon laden with heavy boxes of papers and books.

We began to grasp what was happening when we could hear and more or less see a turbulent horde of shouting, angry men pouring out of Hampton City at a hard gallop. We saw flash after flash and heard report after report. They were shooting as wildly as they were riding and the shots were coming our direction. The intended targets obviously were the only fathers we had and the four other men riding with them.

Of course, they were far out of range of our fathers and their treasure at that point. But saddle horses would soon overtake a team pulling a wagon. Our dads would be in range of their rifles, even their six-guns before long.

With Dad driving and Mr. Fullmer urging the horses on, the wagon with the four riders at its side came roaring past us, following the trail between the hole in the ground and the horse weeds that reached over to the old corral. Thank heavens we were adequately hidden so our fathers didn't see us. They had enough on their hands without worrying about their kids caught in a drunken gun fight.

Naturally, it was beginning to cross our minds that we ought to be getting out of there ourselves. Yet, we were more worried about our dads. Those drunken gunmen didn't know about us, but they sure were after our fathers and closing the ground altogether too quickly.

"Quick, Becky, our ropes," I whispered as a plan took root.

I no sooner said it than she squealed in instant recognition, "You're right!"

She twirled her loop once, then flicked it unerringly around a shaft of masonry that was all that remained of the chimney in the old store. We pulled the noose tight, then crawled quickly to the end of the rope, but it wasn't long enough to stretch across the full expanse that the riders would likely cover.

"Hand me your rope," she commanded urgently.

Quickly we tied my lariat onto Becky's and yanked on it, testing the knot to be sure it would hold. The double length of rope was plenty long enough. In fact, it put us on the edge of the horseweeds, which would give us needed protection for a hasty getaway.

And so we had a perfect trip wire as a little surprise for our fathers' belligerent pursuers.

If only they'll stick to the trail and follow the route our fathers had taken, we were hoping. Don't go on the other side of the hole in the ground toward the railroad tracks, we half-prayed.

We dug in with all our might. We planted the heels of our boots firmly in the ground and stretched back until we were almost parallel with the earth, using all of our weight to hold the rope tight against the tons of horseflesh we hoped would hit it. We soon had our answer as the rope jerked and yanked. Horses started falling in a terrified bunch and men went flying through the air, yelling in angry surprise.

Profanity reigned. Drunken curses were hurled into the Saturday night darkness as the crowd from Hampton City wound up in one big squirming, yelling heap. They were shouting at each other, cursing their luck, blaming other men or their horses and continuing to shoot at nowhere in particular.

One drunken soul was so mad that he shot his horse. "Stupid critter," he snarled as he did in the innocent beast.

It wasn't the horse's fault. But the quick trigger finger underscored the point to Becky and me that it was high time to travel. Get out of there fast. We had done our work. We ducked into a well-known path in our horseweed forest and headed for our horses.

We were trying to remain silent and make haste at the same time. But apparently someone heard us. Or maybe one of our horses whinnied. With all the gunfire and other noise our horses probably were jumpy. "Over there," we heard a voice shout.

We could make out the shapes of a couple of men picking themselves up and, with guns in hand, heading in our general direction.

Even cold sober and in broad daylight, they couldn't have penetrated the horseweed thicket except very slowly, shoving the forest aside as they tried to enter it. We knew that. Since they weren't cold sober and it wasn't daylight, all they did was flail away at the long-stemmed weeds while we ran through our trail to our horses.

We heard the curses that were hurled at us. "Come out of there, you dirty bastards." "I'll finish you sons of bitches off the minute I lay hands on you." Things like that. It didn't do much for our morale but it certainly added to our momentum. They also kept shooting, apparently where they thought they heard noise. The noise no doubt was us, maybe just from our hearts pounding. We knew that a bullet could penetrate horse weeds a whole lot easier than men could. Thus, our minds concentrated in full terror on the prospect of a wild shot finding its mark as we made a final, panicky sprint to our horses.

The horses too, were close to panic. They were pulling hard on the reins tied to the old corral. As soon as we got them untied, we were off at a full gallop even before we were firmly in our saddles. They needed no urging from us.

As soon as we took off, we were out of the cover of the horseweeds. While the horses were putting distance between us and the armed mob fast, we nonetheless were now the open targets of angry shouts and angry shots. It sometimes seemed that we could feel bullets penetrating, although after the fact we realized that nothing had come so close that we could even hear it. We kept pushing the horses, though, long after we were out of range. We weren't about to stick around long enough to let them take aim.

At a hard, full gallop we raced across familiar territory in the dim prairie starlight with no one in pursuit. The fallen were still trying to untangle their horses when we left them to their fate.

We galloped to our place to find an unexpected glow out by the barn. We pulled up to see our fathers, our mothers and the four riders all busy by lantern light. The only ones missing were the younger children. They must have been left in the house, maybe even asleep.

Given a welcome and unexpected break from the armed gang chasing them, the six members of the Sierra Mesa rescue party availed themselves of the opportunity to take a side trip to our home to relieve a pair of overworked horses. A fresh team was being hitched up now to complete the journey to Sierra Mesa. In relative peace, everyone hoped.

"Where have you been?" demanded my dad.

"Where have you been?" insisted Becky's dad.

"Where have you been?" asked my worried mom.

"Where have you been?" Becky's equally worried mom wanted to know.

The questions of course tumbled one on top of the other in rapid fire. Afterward, Becky and I agreed that we had often been asked that question by our parents, but never had had the same question been fired at us by four parents at once.

It did occur to us that we had just received quite a vote of confidence from our parents. They weren't really worried about us, even though we were out later than we were supposed to be. They knew we were totally familiar with the territory. Otherwise they would have been gathering a search party to go looking for us rather than preparing to complete the presentation of county bounty to Sierra Mesa.

Before we could either mumble or blurt out an answer to

the common parental question, my dad's eye fell on an empty strap on my saddle. "What'd you do with your rope?"

His query prompted Becky's dad to glance at her saddle. "And your rope?" he demanded.

Then the two old buckaroos shot each other a knowing glance. The reason for their lucky break out there amid the violence instantly dawned on them as they fixed their attention on the absent lariats. By the dim light of the lanterns, we could see their eyes brighten and they put strong, loving arms around their delinquent children.

Our moms were still in the dark. They only knew that their men had escaped a harrowing ordeal in which they were shot at and now needed a fresh team to go the rest of the way to town. Their oldest children had been out much too late and weren't getting so much as a reprimand from their fathers.

They hadn't thought of what the penalty should be and they weren't sure that their husbands ought to continue that night. But they did know that their children's behavior ought to be punished and they also knew they didn't want the disputed baggage to be left where it was, lest it stand as an invitation for angry armed men to come calling.

"Seems it wasn't just luck that tripped up the boys from Hampton City," Mr. Fullmer said, looking proudly on his daughter.

"We didn't know why those horses toppled all over the place," Dad said. "We didn't stop to find out. We just thanked our lucky stars and kept going.

"But I'd allow as how it wasn't no simple thing like the lead horse hit a badger hole and the rest fell on top of him."

Becky's dad grinned. "Nope. Reckon if we was to go out there we might find a couple of lariats tied together that were stretched about a foot off the ground when them fellers come through."

Becky and I glanced at each other with knowing smiles and snuggled closer in our fathers' strong arms.

Our mothers caught on fast. No lucky stars saved their men. If luck were involved, it involved naughty children being out too late and being where they didn't belong. There wasn't a dose of punishment to be had, not even a mild admonition. Instead our mothers merely broke out the apple pie later when we went into the house as our fathers and their horsemen headed toward town with a fresh team taking its time to get them and their county cargo to their destination.

It turned out that three of the men from Hampton City eventually got their horses on their feet and decided to proceed to Sierra Mesa. The others didn't. In addition to the one who shot his horse, some others were left afoot by injured horses, some of which unfortunately might have to be destroyed. For the remainder, the fight was gone. They just wanted to get back to finish their Saturday night routine before the hangover set in prematurely.

Meanwhile, worry time had arrived for the men of Sierra Mesa who stayed behind to give support when the wagon with the valuable goods came into view.

You could enter Sierra Mesa at either the north or south end of a wandering street that started out as a horse trail years before. The town grew up north and south as a result of it. The plan was for the wagon coming from Hampton City to the west would enter Sierra Mesa at its northern gateway. But where was it?

"They shoulda been here by now," said Henry Guzman. "Something's gone haywire. I know it."

The sound of hoof beats brought the armed band to its feet, guarding the northern entrance while keeping their focus to the west, toward Hampton City.

There were three of them. And they definitely were not the Sierra Mesa men who went on the mission. This wasn't good.

The three riders, all that was left of the hastily assembled mob from the saloon in Hampton City, found themselves staring into rifle barrels in all directions.

"What do you boys want?" demanded Guzman.

"We're looking for a gang of thieves that stole the county."

"What'd you do with them?"

"What do you mean, what did we do with them?"

The three heard levers clicking and cartridges slamming into chambers.

"You boys get down off your horses, put down your weapons and start talking real fast about what you did to some mighty good men."

Three interlopers were as puzzled by the conversation as were the Sierra Mesa men who demanded answers about their missing cohorts. The three were as sure that the wagon load of precious loot was now in Sierra Mesa as the others were that their compatriots had been waylaid somewhere.

All were startled by a noise that came from behind them, to the south. A wagon accompanied by four riders crawled into view.

Guzman and others recognized the scene. There were Dad, Mr. Fullmer and the others, but he was perplexed. They were late, but seemed unhurried, and they were coming in from the wrong direction.

"What happened, Ben? You were supposed to come down the road this way from the west and you were supposed to do it maybe an hour or so ago."

"We got caught, Henry," Dad explained. "We had a bunch of drunken yahoos comin' after us and shootin' at us and by the time we got away from them we needed fresh horses."

"So we stopped at Ben's place." Ted Fullmer took over. "After we hitched up a new team we just thought we'd come up from the south and reduce the risk of running into any stragglers from Hampton City like the three you seem to have for company here."

"You going to let us go now?" asked one of the three.

"And let us take our rightful property with us?" chimed in another. The first shot him a wary look. He'd settle for his neck right now and worry about boxes of papers later.

"Rightful property," Henry Guzman scoffed. "You're coming with us."

The three, hands tied behind their back, were marched into downtown Sierra Mesa where Saturday night revelers hanging around the saloons gave them puzzled looks and occasional drunken hoots.

The trio recognized Ed Duggin's saloon as they approached it. It was clear to them Duggin's place was their destination. For a second they permitted themselves the thought that perhaps they were among generous hosts who would have a Saturday night drink with them as evidence of no hard feelings and send them on their way.

Then they saw Duggin's freshly repainted sign: Hunkapapa Saloon and County Courthouse.

The word "county" was new to the old sign and kind of squished in where there really wasn't a place for it. The bottom line had been repainted for the first time in many years. It now very clearly said "Courthouse" in big, bold, black letters. But when they examined it a bit more closely they could still make out the faded letters that spelled "W-h-o-re" under the newly painted "C-o-u-r-t."

With the whorehouse turned courthouse, Ed Duggin's place had a purpose again. The three guests from Hampton City were ushered into an upstairs room where they heard the door close behind them and a lock click into place.

A week before it came into existence, Hunkapapa County had its first jail inmates.

EIGHT

Oh, my! I'm telling you, the fulmination over the next few days kicked up clouds of dust all over the emerging Hunkapapa County, not to mention Jefferson County, the state Capitol and all the way to Great Lakes Pacific Railroad headquarters in Rensburgh.

Emory G. Pastwell was beside himself with grief, anger and frustration. We could all understand that, although most of us thought he had it coming. The unexpected tragedy was of a magnitude beyond his grasp.

State Representative S. Franklin Pierce had extricated himself as best he could to avoid being drawn into a bloody ruckus pitting his constituents against his constituents. But Pastwell drank himself into a stupor Saturday night while waiting word from the posse, as he thought of it, that he had assembled. Not until the awful haze of the next morning did he learn of the mission's failure.

His simple, little scheme, so certain of success, had been turned against him. The sales gimmick backfired. His county not only had the wrong name, but also it now had the wrong county seat.

He called for every remedy that came to mind. He tried to rally the men of Hampton City to take back the county records by force. But, having suffered a humiliating and painful setback once already when they responded to his cries, they didn't care at all for the chance he offered them to redeem themselves. Besides, he wasn't suggesting that he would lead the charge. He would only hold their coats while they fought his county-seat battle for him.

"Go take 'em back yourself," growled the fellow who had shot his horse in drunken anger. He was still smarting over the loss of a good horse, and was more inclined to blame Pastwell than himself for a senseless act.

Pastwell grabbed the train to Gortonville to pay an urgent call on Sheriff Horace Sharp.

He demanded to see the sheriff himself, not some deputy. Rampant crime in Jefferson County was being ignored. It had to be brought to the attention of the sheriff himself. So, in exasperation, a deputy ushered him into Sheriff Sharp's personal office.

"A bunch of thieves robbed us blind," he bellowed at the sheriff. "And you just sit there. When are you going to get off your duff and do your duty?"

The sheriff looked him over during a long pause. He tipped his hat back, locked his hands behind his neck, settled back in his chair and demanded, "Just what duty you talking about, my friend?"

"Go catch the thieves who robbed the county."

"Whoa, now," Sheriff Sharp said. "Who robbed who? I don't know how one group of citizens can rob another group of citizens when they are fightin' over something that belongs to all of 'em."

"But the county records were in Hampton City. They were

ours. They belong to us. We were robbed right under your nose and you do nothing about it."

The sheriff realized that the area was still technically part of his jurisdiction, but only for a few more days. The issue was a county seat for Hunkapapa County and that was a question for Hunkapapa County to resolve, he reasoned, and best he stay out of it.

"I'm telling you, Mr. Pastwell," the sheriff went on, "there's no way I can tell who was stealing from whom. Under the law, Hampton City has no greater claim to those papers than Sierra Mesa. It is a local argument and I have no business pokin' my nose in."

The arrest and overnight lock-up of the three drunken riders from Hampton City might have been more serious, the sheriff reckoned, because no one had authority to toss them into a makeshift hoosegow. But he said nothing of that concern to Emory Pastwell. No point giving this overwrought constituent more ammunition for his tantrum. And the gun play. The Hampton City crowd shooting at the men from Sierra Mesa, now that was serious indeed. Probably attempted murder. But he didn't mention that either. He would just invite more irrational argument from his irate visitor. He wanted to keep hands off the entire mess.

Pastwell stormed from the sheriff's office and made a beeline to the law office of state Representative S. Franklin Pierce. Pierce owed him plenty. It was time to pay off.

"Well, Emory, nice to see you." The representative greeted him warmly, although, having known about the Hampton City raid, he suspected the visit was not going to be a particularly pleasant one. "What brings you to Gortonville?"

"I'm not here for idle chatter, Franklin," his sometimes buddy shot back. "Tragedy struck Hampton City. We were robbed of our county by a gang of thugs from Sierra Mesa."

"Yes, I'm aware of that little scuffle," the representative allowed. "I was there for the start of it. Remember?"

"Then why in heaven's name, man, haven't you done anything about it?" Pastwell demanded. "We've got a crime wave and you dismiss it as a little scuffle?"

"Well, it is a local dispute, Emory. What would you have me do?"

"Do something. Anything. Get the legislature back in session and declare Hampton City county seat like you originally had it. That was the whole reason for the county and you didn't even get the right name on it. You owe me, Pierce. You owe me three hundred dollars worth of action."

Owe. That ill-advised comment brought the matter of the purchase of political influence right out into the open, which was courting disaster. Pierce was disturbed, but he struggled to maintain his calm.

"The legislature is adjourned. Special sessions are rare and only called for greater emergencies than this, Emory. I can assure you that the governor could not be expected to call one."

"Then get him to call out the militia and march those records right back where they belong."

"The militia? Come now, Emory. I know how important this is to you. But it hardly calls for war."

"They waged war on us, didn't they? Its an armed insurrection and the state should fight back."

"Take it easy, Emory," the representative urged. "It was not war. It was a local dispute. It is serious. But it simply does not call for the militia."

"All right, if you won't do that at least go to court," Pastwell implored. "After all, Hampton City was declared county seat in the governor's order. Make the court enforce the order."

"I would caution against that, Emory. The courts have a record of staying out of local fracases over the location of the county courthouse even when the competition turned hostile. This isn't the first time gunfire was involved in a dispute over the county seat, you know."

"But," implored Pastwell, "it's in the governor's order."

"The governor's order names Hampton City as the temporary county seat. Put emphasis on temporary. I can tell you what a court would do. The judge would order an immediate election to determine a permanent county seat. That's what they always do. I'm going to warn you if you gotta go to an election, you can't win anyway," the lawyer-representative advised his client-constituent. "Your only hope is to take back the records and hold them in your courthouse until people get used to the idea. And you'll have to try to prevent an election."

For the second time that day Emory G. Pastwell stomped out of an official's office in Gortonville.

Pierce was somewhat relieved. He was growing weary of his rich friend, whom he was beginning to suspect was not what he seemed. Bringing out in the open the matter of money paid for political favor was something that violated all of the rules of trust and honor.

Well, so what. Pierce had milked Pastwell and the GLP for about all he could expect. Time was at hand for cutting losses and moving on to the next opportunity for political power and personal wealth.

Pastwell headed for the GLP depot to send a telegram to his powerful brother-in-law, Otis P. Hampton, the assistant vice president of the Great Lakes Pacific Railroad.

> COUNTY SEAT IN JEOPARDY STOP LAWLESSNESS WIDESPREAD STOP RIOTERS STOLE RECORDS STOP SIERRA MESA HAS THEM STOP NEED HELP QUICK STOP.

In Pastwell's frame of mind, his wire may not even have been an exaggeration. Rioting. Widespread lawlessness. That's about the way he pictured the dire circumstances.

Otis P. Hampton was dumbfounded by the telegram. He puzzled over it trying to make out what had happened. Had his brother-in-law actually fouled up a deal so certain that it could not fail? What happened?

He decided to take decisive action first and learn more of what happened later. If the situation was anywhere close to the tone of his brother-in-law's telegram, there was no time for facts. His wire to the governor in the name of the Great Lakes Pacific Railroad demanded gubernatorial intervention, including calling out the militia if needed.

The governor hardly wanted to cross the powerful railroad. However, if anything so dreadful had resulted that the militia were needed he surely would know it by now. He suspected it was just another local squabble over siting the county seat of a new county.

Nonetheless, to be sure, he dispatched his chief aide to Hunkapapa County-to-be. He might be called executive assistant or chief of staff today, but then he was simply called the governor's secretary and was just about all the staff the governor had.

The secretary found bruised feelings in Hampton City, but little more than that, other than an obnoxious Emory G. Pastwell, whose demands were outrageous: "Tell that governor to call out the militia now and take the county records back by force."

The records clearly were in Sierra Mesa, but so what? He went on to Gortonville to consult with Representative Pierce.

"I'd stay out of it if I were the governor," the representative advised. "It's one of those local controversies that can only be settled locally. The governor couldn't win if he got involved. Politically, it would be a disaster for him and he doesn't need that."

"That will be my report to the governor," said the secretary and returned to the Capitol to offer the advice to a much relieved governor.

The governor assured Assistant Vice President Hampton by wire that there were no riots, no need for the militia, nothing but a local dispute that did not involve the state.

Hampton wasn't happy but knew there was nothing else he could do with the governor. So he simply wired his no-account brother-in-law:

GOVERNOR WON'T ACT STOP YOU'RE ON YOUR OWN STOP TAKE WHATEVER ACTION YOU MUST STOP.

Pastwell had heard about a county down in Kansas where the two rival towns both were trying to build courthouses, but each kept burning down the one erected by the other.

He put the word out in Hampton City for an arson contract. But the hungover trio of jailbirds had dampened any enthusiasm for such a project.

They rode home Sunday morning after their release from the makeshift jail with the report of just where the county was housed. The newly converted courthouse out of the old whorehouse was deep in the heart of Sierra Mesa. It was about as invulnerable to attack by Hampton City as a building could be. There may have been men in Hampton City willing to torch Ed Duggin's saloon if they thought they could get away with it, but none willing to face the odds.

Taking no chances, the men of Sierra Mesa took turns guarding their prize. They had at least two armed and ready at all times. And it was just as well that they did.

Late one night one of them spotted a fellow poking about the rear of the Hunkapapa Saloon and County Courthouse. He advised Ed Duggin and the other guard. They hadn't recognized Emory Pastwell at first, for he was dressed in common attire. But they caught him with a container of lamp oil, a bunch of rags, and a box of matches as he pondered how one goes about setting a building on fire.

Over his protests that he was within his constitutional rights to be where he was and doing what he was doing, they hustled him to their jail room and unceremoniously tossed him in. Then they contemplated what to do with him.

The truth as they pondered it was that they had not caught him committing a crime even though it was apparent he was about to do so. And they really didn't have any authority because the Hunkapapa District was not yet a county; nor was one of them a sheriff with the power of law behind him.

The next morning they let Pastwell go, but with a stern warning:

"You show your face in Sierra Mesa again and we will build a gallows to string you up so fast you won't have time to say your prayers."

They marched him to the edge of town and he was left afoot to make his way the eleven miles back to Hampton City.

The only alternative was to sit on the tracks and hope to be able to flag down the westbound GLP train in the afternoon. Since the engineer was not accustomed to flag stops, that was a doubtful tactic. He walked.

By this time, Pastwell was alone in his struggle for action. Oh, the folks in Hampton City he had recruited were sympathetic, but there wasn't much they could do. They were outnumbered by Sierra Mesa and the town's rancher friends. Clearly it would do their interests no good at all to put the question of a county seat on the ballot to be decided by voters. And the odds were stacked against them that they could decide it in their favor in any other way.

The men of Sierra Mesa were still on guard on Saturday when Hunkapapa formally became a county. Thus, for the second weekend in a row a large contingent of men stayed sober to guard against a counterattack.

"Gettin' mighty tired of this damned county business," grumbled Ed Duggin as he saw his Saturday night take vastly reduced twice in two Saturdays. He counted on that Saturday night spree for most of his profits.

But it was good-natured grumbling. Over time he knew he could count on business the county would generate to make him a pile of money. Meanwhile, the courthouse gave him something that he found every bit as much to his liking as wealth. It gave him respect. His old whorehouse had been transformed from a point of shame to a point of pride in his community.

Matrons of Sierra Mesa, including those who got their introduction to the town by plying their time-tested trade in those upstairs rooms, no longer looked on the building with embarrassment, a reminder of a rowdy past the civilized community no longer wished to be associated with. Ed Duggin had indeed performed a valuable civic duty by making unused and unwanted space available for the county.

By the time the appointed county clerk arrived on Friday to take charge of the new county the following day, he went to Sierra Mesa without hesitation.

As the eastbound train stopped in Hampton City en route from the capital city to Sierra Mesa, Pastwell boarded to plead that the clerk remain in Hampton City and demand that the records be brought to him, but the clerk pointed out, "It's not my place to say where the records are kept. Its my job to preside over the records wherever they may be."

So Hunkapapa County got under way with Sierra Mesa as its seat. Hampton City had in effect given up. Emory Pastwell was no longer much of a threat. That left only one matter to attend do: The special election to be held in two months to choose the three commissioners, the sheriff, a treasurer, an auditor, an assessor, a permanent clerk, and the county surveyor.

Henry Guzman assembled the dozen men who had planned the successful raid. They gathered again in Ed Duggin's saloon, six from the town, six from the country.

"Our work is not done," he said. "Now we have to assure the election. We need to be sure we elect a friendly commission. Otherwise, after all we've gone through, the commission could pack up the county records and take them to Hampton City and that would be that. Our only hope then would be to try to force an election. But once things got settled in Hampton City, who knows how that would come out?"

They needed balance, the group thought. They needed to mesh political differences as well as regional variety.

"Why don't we talk to Jim Hickock?" my dad, Ben Baxter suggested. "I hear he won't run for the Senate again. But wouldn't he be something as the first chairman of our county commission?"

The group reacted as if all should have thought of it first. They would approach Jim Hickock, draft him if they had to. They would have an authentic hero. Everyone knew of the prominent role he played in acquiring statehood.

Then they turned to Henry Guzman. He protested. "There are younger, abler men for the job."

But his associates insisted. "You're the right one from town. Lots of folks think of you as the founder of Sierra Mesa. They naturally turned to you to be the first mayor. They'll just as naturally turn to you again."

Reluctantly, he agreed to serve once more if they wanted him.

"And I nominate Ben Baxter from the country," Ted Fullmer said.

"Me? Why me?" my dad answered. "I ain't no politician. Never gave a speech in my life. Why not you?"

"'Cause I got to you before you got to me," his friend and neighbor chuckled.

And so they had their ticket. Mr. Guzman was a Republican. Dad and Senator Hickock were Democrats. But more than anything, Dad was a Populist. That was fine. Political differences could be aired later when the county was on sound footing. Right now they needed balance.

The rest of the group stuck together to try to persuade other supporters of Sierra Mesa to stay out of the election this time. They could run later. Or they could run for one of the many other offices. But right now the best thing they could do was to stick with the slate for the first commission.

Voters could vote for three candidates and the three with the most votes would be elected, whether they had a majority or not. A solid slate looked like the best strategy. Package them as a team and have them campaign together.

Emory Pastwell scraped up some candidates from Hampton City in a feeble attempt to win what he still saw as his right. But his cause did look hopeless in an honest election. To try to avoid honesty from interfering with the democratic process, he did his level best to smear the team from Sierra Mesa. Indeed, he concentrated more of his energy on the mudslinging campaign than on promoting his candidates.

"They're nothing but common criminals," he bellowed to a handful of Hampton City residents who gathered in the town square for what passed as a political rally.

When someone in the audience, who wanted to believe if he could be given credible evidence, asked for an example, the only thing he could stick them with the participation by Dad and Mr. Guzman in taking the records. Folks throughout the county, even in Hampton City, hardly saw that as criminal behavior. Anyway, one of the three, Senator Hickock, wasn't even involved in the operation.

He tried to make my dad out a philanderer. When pressed for an example by his Hampton City editor who was only trying to be helpful, Pastwell accused Dad of running around with Sally Fullmer.

It made Dad so mad he threatened to quit. "I've had it up to here with this politics." He spat out the offensive term.

"You can't quit," Mom said. "That would just confirm it in some people's minds, who know better as it is."

"But what do I do about it? What do I say?"

"Mainly ignore it," Mom suggested.

"But what if it keeps coming up?"

"Deny it emphatically and move on. Just say, 'Utterly ridiculous.'"

"Utterly ain't a word I use," Dad protested.

"It is now, Lover. Say it."

"Utterly ridiculous."

"Sound indignant. Put a little bite in it," Mom directed.

Dad leveled a stare at her, tightened his lips, and snapped, "Utterly ridiculous."

"That's it," Mom said. "But I really don't think you'll have to use it. Everybody knows you better than that."

"I hope so."

"And if they don't, they know Sally better than that," Mom added.

"Yeah. She'd never have anything to do with anyone but Ted," Dad agreed.

"And if they don't, they know me better than that," she declared.

"How's that?"

"You're not walking around with a knot on your head, are you?"

"No," Dad agreed. "So?"

"So everyone knows if you so much as looked at another woman I'd crown you with the first skillet I could get my hands on."

Then she kissed him, hard. She was only joking, but in earnest.

Mom was right. Everybody did indeed seem to know better than Emory G. Pastwell's phony issue. His demagoguery was so crude it just made him look all the worse.

He was so desperate he even tried to label Henry Guzman a homosexual. When the storekeeper heard about it, it struck him so funny he didn't bother to get upset about it. Here he was a devout Roman Catholic with nine children to show for it and the very picture of a dedicated family man. The Guzmans, as the whole community knew, had so many grandchildren that most folks lost count. Now they even had great-grandchildren.

"If anybody wants to ask about it," Henry Guzman said, "I'm going to tell them, 'I don't know what that has to do with my qualifications for county commissioner, but if you are concerned about my sexuality I refer you to the only expert witness on the subject, Mrs. Guzman.'"

But he didn't have to use the line, much to the relief of his wife who was beside herself with embarrassment when she heard of his proposed tactic. She knew him well enough to know that he just might employ it.

And when the hapless demagogue called Jim Hickock a corrupt politician on the take in the state Senate, he almost got laughed out of the county. If anything, Hickock had earned a widespread reputation as being overly straight.

The three came up with a symbol for the campaign in the form of a brand. They took an *H* for Hickock and tacked on a *G* for Guzman to the inside of the upper left upright of the letter and a *B* for Baxter inside the lower left.

"The right brand for Hunkapapa County," their material said. The ticket was elected by a wide margin. Pastwell's desperate tactics probably helped it.

The first commission took Ed Duggin's old whorehouse and divided up the rooms. They found office space for each of the other elected officials. They fixed up a room for the commissioners to meet in and another for the circuit judge to use for a courtroom when he came to town. And they kept one for a jail, the one that already had seen service for that purpose.

For the first couple of years until they could scrape together enough votes to approve building a real brick courthouse, the old whorehouse over Duggin's saloon did just fine.

Hunkapapa County was off and running with Sierra Mesa firmly established as county seat.

NINE

While Sierra Mesa was taking off, Hampton City was on the decline. Emory Pastwell and his highly placed brother-in-law, Otis Hampton, were right about one thing: There was need for only one town in Hunkapapa County and that town obviously would be the county seat.

So, the loss of the county seat turned out to be the finish for Hampton City. No one was interested any more. Emory Pastwell was frantic. He did his best to undo the damage, but the shift of county records to Sierra Mesa had had the effect of exposing Hampton City as a hocus town.

People who had been interested in the building of a new city suddenly saw it as a sham that had no purpose other than to make an eastern dandy rich and kill off an established town as a result. Hampton City stood as little more than a monument to greed.

Pastwell had spent his last cent, indeed the last of his credit, on throwing together the wooden building he had intended as the first courthouse. It sat vacant, never used, in the square across from the depot.

And sometime Emory G. Pastwell simply disappeared. No one saw him go or knew where he went. In marked contrast to the arrival of a Chicago peddler with high top hat and long morning coat, he just vanished. His parting was as inconspicuous as his arrival had been conspicuous.

Was it possible that Otis P. Hampton, the assistant vice president of the Great Lakes Pacific Railroad, had carried out his initial threat? Pastwell would take good care of his wife, the assistant vice president's sister, or disappear forever at the competent hands of the bullies who served the railroad as detectives.

Well, he certainly wasn't taking very good care of his wife after Hampton City collapsed. His brother-in-law might have concluded that, even after being handed a sure thing, the worthless husband of his sister wasn't equal to the task and therefore wasn't worth the bother of keeping around. He would never be anything but a burden.

Or Pastwell, looking at the worst of all possible worlds, might have gambled that a quick change of scenery and a new identity were his best hope to salvage some happiness in life and shield him from his brother-in-law's frightful pledge. After all, he was both broke and married. The gamble might have been worth it. Nothing could be worse than that, not even the railroad detectives.

After hearing nothing for more than a month, Emily Hampton Pastwell finally came out on a GLP train herself to look for her husband, leaving her young daughter behind with her grandmother. But Emory Pastwell did not magically reappear when his wife arrived. The local people were polite and sympathetic, but they were no help to her because no one knew anything about his whereabouts. Not a soul knew where he was; not a soul had seen him go.

Kindly, state Representative S. Franklin Pierce was only

too willing to offer his assistance to the grieving wife—or widow. Upon seeing the glamorous spouse of his former friend, he extended his services as escort to go looking for the missing man.

His real strategy was simple, with Emily Pastwell as the prize. But it was elaborately disguised:

"We will go to every town along the railroad. We'll take a picture and description of the man with us. We will question every community in detail until we get wind of his whereabouts. He can't just drop out of sight. He's depressed, no doubt about it, but he's around somewhere and it's a good bet we'll find him along the GLP line somewhere."

Emily Pastwell was much relieved. She had been all alone in a hostile world, no one else caring enough to help her. She now had a pillar of strength to lean on, someone who knew what he was doing.

They boarded a train and headed west. Pierce's ruse was convincing. He was about as determined to find the missing Mr. Pastwell as he was to leave the lovely Mrs. Pastwell alone in her misery. But his act could have fooled many a person in a less emotional state than Emily Hampton Pastwell.

She had every reason to believe that he was searching diligently. At each town where the train stopped, he would take his leave to make inquiry of the local people. The nearby saloon was the most likely place to find a gathering of people who might have some knowledge of a stranger. So he would go to the saloon, have a quiet drink, and come back announcing that he had asked in great detail about his absent friend. He also returned with whiskey, to be dispensed in medicinal quantities, you understand, to help Mrs. Pastwell cope with her depression and calm her nerves.

What a nice man to do this for her; he was such a comfort, Emily Hampton Pastwell thought to herself. Oh, she was so grateful for his earnest endeavors and his thoughtful companionship. It was a relief to have such a friend in an hour of need.

Grateful enough, indeed, that with the aid of a few medicinal quantities of whiskey, the dosage of which became systematically larger, she understood this kind man's concern about leaving her alone in a strange hotel in a rough-and-tumble little city on the hurly-burly frontier.

It may be an overstatement to say that she understood. The medicine she had received left her with considerably impaired judgment. Indeed, it was about all she could do to walk when they finally left the train after a long day's ride, because Franklin had told her she needed a better night's sleep than she could get on the train.

He had to steady her as he checked them into the nearby hotel. By the time he maneuvered them to their room, she was absolutely giddy. And as soon as she threw her arms around him in a tight embrace and giggled, she passed out.

Pierce had not laid his careful plans to get this beauty alone in a hotel room just to hold her hand while she slept off a binge. He proceeded to unclothe her. She cooed contentedly when he nibbled her nipples and fondled her nude body. By the time he entered her, she had come to, however vaguely, and she squealed with delight. She was conscious enough to exult in the moment of ecstasy, but the name she spoke was Emory.

As she was coming out of her stupor a few hours later and felt strong arms around her, she again murmured, "Emory." Then she sat up and gasped in a mixture of realization and denial, "EMORY?"

"No, my beloved. It is your ever-faithful Franklin," the man sharing her bed announced.

"Franklin?" she asked, then, "FRANKLIN!," as she forced herself to face the fact that his companionship had been extended to the long night in a strange hotel out on the frontier.

She hoisted bedding over her exposed breasts, but his strong arms gently yet firmly pulled her to him again and she soon let the tension drain away. She was caught up in the three *H*s of the morning after—hungover, hungry and horny. He soon tended to the latter. Again the name she uttered was Emory.

But that was the last time she did so. She felt too ill to travel, so they spent the day in the hotel. Pierce brought in food and also a few doses of last night's medicine to help her recover. By evening, as she was feeling better, she also was losing interest in finding her husband and gaining interest in her dashing benefactor with the remarkable bedroom skills.

Indeed, as Hampton City began to deteriorate into the ghost town it is today, Franklin Pierce was managing to weasel his way up the political ladder. From the place in the state Senate he acquired when Jim Hickock did not run again, he collected enough dirt on his fellow legislators along with political IOUs, adding some cash when further inducement was needed, to secure a seat in the U.S. Senate.

His glamorous lady, so bored with the ways of Rensburgh, found the glitz of Washington society to be custom made for her tastes. Senator Pierce made it a point to introduce her as Mrs. Pierce, although no one was ever aware that she had acquired either a divorce or certification of her husband's death, or bothered to exchange vows with Senator Pierce.

The big money and opportunity for corruption in the U. S. Senate were almost too much even for Franklin Pierce's appetite. Chances to obtain money in return for political favor were so plentiful, Pierce hardly knew where to grab next.

It was whispered around the social circles of Washington that his senatorial service was so marked by avarice and ambition that he had a great deal to do with approval of the Seventeenth Amendment to the Constitution. The amendment required selection of United States senators by popular voter instead of the state legislature.

When the amendment was approved in 1913, Pierce's political career was over. But he didn't return home. He and the lady known as Mrs. Pierce, and her daughter, Deborah, who also went by Pierce, stayed in Washington where he acquired wealth doing whatever it took to peddle influence. Lobbyists who plied their trade by the rules didn't know how he did it, but somehow he was wily enough that he even stayed out of jail.

In Rensburgh, the rapid ascendancy of Otis P. Hampton toward the top of the Great Lakes Pacific Railroad came to an abrupt halt. Oh, he remained with the company, but the Hampton City fiasco was such a great loss to the railroad in both money and prestige that he never got the "assistant" modifier erased from his title.

As Becky and I approach our 50th anniversary, still helping our children run both the Fullmer and Baxter spreads, we look back on that wacky year in the best of times and the worst of times when the tale of two small towns unfolded. We think of a couple of crazy kids in a hole in the ground and a forest of horseweeds.

We sometimes just break out laughing about it, yet we wonder what would have happened if those kids hadn't had a couple of ropes pulled tight across a trail one night long ago.

Hampton City, once intended to become the principal city in this part of the country, is just a pile of dilapidated shacks now. The last of the people who lived there moved out a few years ago. The intended courthouse never was used for anything and it still sags there among the weeds in the town square ready to topple into itself one of these days.

But Sierra Mesa prospers, at least as much as small trade towns can in ranching country these days. Its stores are still busy, although there aren't as many as there were at its peak. Good roads and good cars have made it easier for folks to go to larger cities for some of their trade, which takes away from small market towns like Sierra Mesa a little. But the town still serves a special need, marked most notably by the red brick courthouse, which remains the dominant fixture downtown.

A fire broke out in Ed Duggin's old saloon and whorehouse long ago during prohibition when it was sitting empty. It didn't do a lot of damage, but it made people think about how close they had come to losing an edifice of their history. The community held enough bake sales to restore it and its sign now says "Hunkapapa County Museum." But the old sign designating it the Hunkapapa Saloon and County Courthouse is on display inside. If you look closely you can still make out the faded lettering w-h-o-r-e under c-o-u-r-t.

Hunkapapa County is so small in population that it probably wouldn't be created today. But it still serves a purpose. Those of us who live here are glad we don't have to go to

Gortonville to tend to county business.

Besides, whether it ought to be a separate county or not, it is and will be. Funny how when we were kids the legislature routinely created counties every two years. Now if modern legislators so much as thought of changing a county boundary, the only thing they would ever run for again is the state line. It's as if those invisible barriers were carved in stone.

Sierra Mesa never has given names to its streets. The old ones, the originals, are still kind of funny, running this way and that the way the horse trails developed right after Henry Guzman put up his country store with the Spanish oxymoron for its fancy name.

One thing has changed. There are five churches now and only three bars. But Saturday nights are still Saturday nights and it is still hard to get some of the imbibers out for redemption on Sunday morning.

As for Becky and me, of course we were destined to get married. Who else could there have been for either of us? But after all of these years, we remain more than anything else, close pals. A few horseweeds still grow straight and tall along the creek by the old corral, but we sometimes long for the profusion of old when they served effectively as a forest. We'd probably still be out there carving trails in the spring.

If it hadn't been for a trail through the horseweeds, there might not be a Sierra Mesa today.